Benjamin F. Taylor

Pictures of Life in Camp and Field

Benjamin F. Taylor

Pictures of Life in Camp and Field

ISBN/EAN: 9783337057671

Printed in Europe, USA, Canada, Australia, Japan

Cover: Foto ©Raphael Reischuk / pixelio.de

More available books at **www.hansebooks.com**

PICTURES OF LIFE

IN

CAMP AND FIELD.

BY

AUTHOR OF "ATTRACTIONS OF LANGUAGE," "OLD TIME PICTURES,"
"THE WORLD ON WHEELS," ETC., ETC.

SECOND EDITION.

CHICAGO:
S. C. GRIGGS & COMPANY.
1875.

LETTER LIST.

LETTER LIST.

ON THE THRESHOLD.

A FEW fragments of old letters compose this volume. They are not in disguise. They wear the every-day apparel of first expression just as it was fashioned at the Front. They are to a chapter or two of History only what the work of the wood-engraver is to the printed page—just a few pictures to brighten the well-considered utterances of the historic Muse.

Written some years ago to the Chicago Evening Journal, thousands who lent them life or gave them heed have passed away. But the deeds have not perished; the story remains; the pictures are undimmed. Illustrating American manhood, those deeds are the heritage of all the people.

One bright day in May, a year ago, the author stood in Rose Hill Cemetery, Chicago, between the quick and the dead. Pausing on the threshold of this little book he is standing between the living and the dead

once more, and he thinks the same thought and says
the same words:

We have come into court, this court of the Lord,
To bear witness for them that can utter no word.
Bare-hearted and browed in this presence we stand,
For the gift Pentecostal comes down on the land ;
To speak for the speechless·how witnesses throng,
And the earth is all voice, and the air is all song !
There's a fleet of white ships blown abroad on the deep,
And their courses forever they peacefully keep,
And they toss us a roar and it melts into words,
And they strike to the heart like the sweeping of swords :
" Would ye honor the men you must look in their graves,
Who did score danger out with their wakes from the waves."
There are soft, fleecy clouds fast asleep in the sun,
Like a flock of white sheep when the washing is done,
Not a breath of a battle is staining the blue,
It is nothing but Paradise all the way through !
There are domes of white blossoms where swelled the white tent,
There are plows in the field where the war wagons went,
There are songs where they lifted up Rachel's lament.
Would you know what this mighty beatitude cost,
You must search in the graves for what Liberty lost !
Ye that trod the acanthus and trampled it down,
And it turned at the touch a Corinthian crown !
Disenthralled from your graves you have left them alone,
We will borrow them now for these dead of our own !
Let us bury all bitterness, passion and pride,
Lay the rankling old wrong to its rest by their side,
Keeping step to the manhood that marches the zone,
And believe the good GOD will take care of His own!

IN CAMP AND FIELD.

FROM ONE WORLD TO ANOTHER.

IT happened to me to follow, for a time, the fortunes of the Army of the Cumberland; not to grasp a musket, but to wield a meaner implement and trifle with a pen. And yet you must believe that some stray nerve of mine felt down its way at last, to that pencil's point, and almost before I knew it, I was writing my heart out in admiration and love for the fortitude and valor of those Federal journeymen of ours, splendid in doing, and grand in suffering.

To pass in forty hours from fields where a thistle is a sin to regions where bayonets sprout as dense as the springing corn in June, is like being born into a new world. If the reader will visit one of the noble Chicago Elevators—those immense houses for a mighty hand to move in, that tosses about the grain as lightly as the farmer sows the seed; if he will watch the golden produce of a broad State received as easily as

Noah, first Admiral of " the red, white and blue," took
in the returning bird; if he will follow that grain to the
snowy loaves and the laden tables of half a continent;
to the tons of white tiles of hard-bread in a thousand
Federal camps; if he will think what a benignant hand
of Providence that Elevator is, and then, if, after all
this, he will fancy an establishment away at the other
extreme of the arc of human invention, as totally
unlike in its office and results as two things can be, and
exist on the same planet, he will have precisely the
place I first blundered into—the Ordnance Depot of
the Army of the Cumberland. If you are given to
glowing words, be dumb; if there be any fire in your
eye, be pleased to shut it while here, among kegs and
barrels of the fine black grain that sows fields with
death; among boxes of cartridges without end; among
rows of canister; among nests of shells, out of which
shall be hatched a terrible brood; among cases of
every species of irritable combustible known in war;
among clusters of the grape that presses the wine of life
out; in the midst of death in every form that flies.
Sentinels stand aside, doors unbolted and unbarred
swing open, a gush of cool air meets you, the shutters
are thrown open, and the treasures of the magazine are
revealed. Wooden boxes of four colors, boxes, boxes,
everywhere—olive, red, black and white. Be seated

upon that olive box; it contains nothing but solid shot, or, perhaps, percussion shell. In the red, you will be sure to find spherical case-shot; in the white boxes, canister; and in the black, that diabolical chronometer, time-shell. Take your choice of a seat and be happy. Look through a glass magnifying about sixty times at an old-fashioned clock-weight, and you will see pretty nearly such a thing as stands there at your right, and which happens to be a hundred-pound " Parrott " shell. A dull affair to look at, but give it a ration of nine pounds of powder and a good range, and it will " make " four miles in twelve seconds at a cost of ten dollars, and possibly something else that it would puzzle you to enter in a cash-book.

Those little round coops, about the size of a lantern, with wooden top and bottom and two wire rings between, contain, as you see, a cluster of nine such grapes as vine-dresser never cultivated. They together weigh eighteen pounds, and by that handle you can swing them about like a dinner-pail. Give a twenty-four-pound gun six pounds of powder and one coop, and that cluster will make nine terrible and deadly lines of flight. We are not well out of the fruit business, for there are thousands of long tin cans, looking home-like and harmless enough to hold the best berry God ever made, that you put up for next Christmas. They are twenty-five pound canisters, filled with shrapnel, five dozen musket-balls, and packed in, like " Isabellas," with saw-dust, as if they were something to " keep." Driven from a thirty-two with eight pounds of powder, your fruit-can goes to pieces, and the bullets scatter as from a tremendous, wide-mouthed musket.

And here we are pleasantly walking where sleeps an earthquake ; making each other hear where slumbers a voice that could shake these everlasting hills.   Ah, what a flash of lightning or a glowing coal could do for all this !   That is not a potash-kettle you have sat down upon—it's a shell !

There are " Parrotts " with their long, black shafts, " reinforced " at the breech, like a trooper's trowsers. There are bright " Napoleons " brisk and spiteful, twelves, twenty-fours, thirty-twos, and so on and so up. Here is a sturdy fellow that growled at Stone River ; there, a grim one that roared at Shiloh ; yonder, a " Columbiad " made at Memphis.   Do you see those pairs of immense wheels?   They are not mill-wheels, but only the carriages of siege-guns.   If it blows at all in this roomy kennel, it must literally " blow great guns."   Those rows of carts with the black boxes and the convex covers are not young bakers' wagons gone into mourning, as you might think, but only battery forges, the blacksmith's shops of Mars' own fiery self.

And so we have seen thunder "in the original package."

GOING TO THE FRONT.

You pass through Kentucky, "the dark and bloody ground," into Tennessee, a beautiful fertile land gone to seed. The villages lie asleep, like lazy dogs, in the sun; stores are closed, shops deserted; through a land dotted with the inkiest imaginable heads, as if some psalm-tune had tumbled out of the score and sprinkled the landscape with Ethiopian rain.

The print of War's fingers is before you. Now you see a gate left standing, by some strange freak, between its two posts—a gate without a fence. And there it swings open upon a path leading to Nowhere! Not a house, not a threshold, only a heap of stone and a blackened tree to tell the story. Now you see the skeleton of a house, if I may call it so; the building stripped of all covering, gaunt and ghastly there in its bones. Now a brick mansion catches the eye; its doors, weary of turning, stand wide open; its garden shivers with weeds; the negro quarters empty, the fields ragged and fenceless as the air, and not a living soul! It may not seem so to you, but I have never felt so heavy a sense of loneliness as when I have seen broad forests of tall corn, the blackened stalks two years old, springing out of earth fairly turfed over and matted, the rusted plow careened in one corner, a wreck on a lee shore; ears of withered corn yet clinging to the russet stems; visions of "hoe-cake" far off and dim; the masters away in the rebel ranks; the "people" strown to the four winds.

As you near the region of the Cumberlands the scenery begins to grow grand; the great, wavy lines of the mountains sweep up bravely toward heaven, and sink down into great troughs of green, but the train makes steadily for the strong horizon; between ledges of God's masonry; through grooves hewn in the rocks, winding this way and that, run the cars. The woods begin to stand up, here and there, like people in a great congregation, as if the spurs of the Cumberland were thrust into the flanks of creation, and it was rousing up to get out of the way of the rowels. An engine comes behind to give us a lift up a prodigious grade of two hundred and fifty feet to the mile. We are going through the mountain. A tunnel, half a mile in length, yawns to swallow us with a throat black as a wolf's mouth. Above it towers the wooded crown, hundreds of feet; close at our right the world seems to make a mis-step and tumble into a deep ravine. A railroad diverges from our track before we reach the tunnel, and runs zigzag over the mountain to a coal-mine, scarring its side with a great letter Z. Up tugs the train to an entrance over which might well be traced, "Those who enter here leave hope behind!" We turn our backs upon a shining sun; it is twilight, night, a darkness that can be felt; it is like putting your eyes out. There is a lull in the steady talk, no laugh comes from the gloom, and so we blunder and thunder through the mountain, and go over the other side, down the camel's back, along a track curved like a sickle, "by the run."

The railroad route from Bridgeport to Chattanooga is one of the wildest and most picturesque on the continent. You make straight at the solid mountain, but creep through a cleft and keep on; you swing around a curve and hang over a gorge, but you play "the devil on two sticks" and pass it; you run like a mouse along a narrow shelf high up the rocky wall, the bewildered Tennessee far beneath, winding this way and that to escape from the enchanted mountains. It flashes out upon you here, curved like a cimeter; it ties the hills up there with love-knots of broad ribbon. The sky line rises and falls around you like a heavy sea; black heaps of coal high up the mountains, look like blots on this roughest of pages in Nature's "writing-book." The dark cedars counterfeit deep shadows. You go through a stone gateway of the Lord's building, and a

deep valley is under your feet. You look far across to
the other side. Will the train run straight out into
mid-air? Will it take wings and fly? It is gliding
cautiously out upon the bridge at Falling Water; the
boys in blue far down, look like drops of indigo; you
are safe over, and you thank God and take courage.
You pass the ruins of hostile camps; the huts are gone,
but the swallow's-nest fire-places remain, and the hill-
sides seem strown with old, rusty honey-comb.

And all along the rugged way, at every station,
bridge, ravine, are rifle-pits and earthworks, the rude
signature rebellion has compelled; grim War's, his †
mark; and all along, those journeymen of ours grouped
to see the train go by; the train, their one, long, slender link with the dear old homes of the North. The
black throats of cannon gape at you over the tops of
their kennels, in unexpected places. The tunes the
drummer beats, all shattered on the crags around, come
tumbling back upon the player's head.

So, through these grand and everlasting halls we
made our way, and when the Morning walked to and
fro upon the top of night, and stepped from height to
height, and pines took fire and cliffs of gray were glorified, it seemed a mighty minster, and I did not wonder
God gave the law from Sinai; that the beatitudes were
shed, like Hermon's dew, from a mountain

Sometimes the valleys widened into fields; garden plats beneath us looked like the squares of a checkerboard, and clusters of poor little dwellings, each lazily smoking a big chimney, seemed having their morning gossip together; now and then, a house was perched high up the mountain, and buzzards, graceful nowhere except in the air, were librating, rocking on their broad wings far below it. A glorious region for painter and poet, whatever plowman may make of it. At last, threading a needle's eye of a tunnel we begin to get into broader ground and the Tennessee bears us company. We wind around the angle of the mountain wall of Lookout; camps glittering on the hills everywhere in the morning sun, tumuli of red earth, with sentinels pacing to and fro, regiments checkering the low grounds, engines backing and filling, great storehouses showing new in their fresh-planed wood, forts dumb but not dead, the whole landscape alive with crowds and caravans. And there in the middle of it all, like a rusty hatchet buried in the live oak that grew around it, lies CHATTANOOGA with its ceaseless eddies of armed life, swords and muskets forever drifting and shifting about in them; good words and bad stirred in together, as if the crowd had been sowed with German, French, English and Ethiopian lexicons, and was just being harvested; "hard tack" and hard talk struggling

in and out together at the same mouths, and hurry
treading on the heels of haste. Upon the sidewalks is
a ceaseless play of blue legs with an unending procession of blue coats; humanity seems done in indigo,
dotted with sutlers, clerks out of livery, correspondents
and faded-out natives. And on all this multitude you
may look all day, and not see one woman of the noble
race that put men upon their honor and make the
world braver and purer. To be sure, there is Aunt
Chloe in turban all afire, like a very sooty chimney red-
hot at the top; and there is Dinah "larding the lean
earth" and looking as if Goodyear might have a
patent for her among his rubber goods; and there too
is a colorless native from the rural districts, whom I
saw an hour ago, dressed in white, un-crinolined, un-
flounced, unwashed, as limp as a wet napkin. She
stood by the post-office door apparently spitting at a
mark—tobacco juice at that—and she delivered her fire
with great accuracy.

But it was not that stronghold among the mountains
that I went to see. It was to find the neighbor I had
missed out of the summer-fallow, where I had seen him
plodding year after year, without knowing him at all;
who had been walking through the world in disguise all
his days; whose heart had grown large with the grandest of all loves, that sweeps like a great horizon around
all meaner passion; had turned into a hero in the

twinkling of an eye, as the dead shall be raised ; had put on the martyr's thorny crown with a smile, or had gone up, like the Prophet in a chariot of fire. It was to see the old deeds packed away in history step out from the silent lines of the printed page, and stand unsandaled on the ground, to make room for the new, that have illustrated the year just dead—tangible, earnest, solemn, glorious.

THREE NOVEMBER DAYS.

The smiting of the enemy's crescent front at Mission Ridge on the twenty-third of November, 1863, the capture of Lookout Mountain on the twenty-fourth, and the storming of Mission Ridge on the twenty-fifth, were really the three acts of one splendid Drama. The letters describing them are placed upon these pages, perhaps unwisely, just as they were written—dim and imperfect pictures taken by the flash of great guns. The play was grand, but what could be grander than

THE THEATRE.

SUNDAY—TWENTY-SECOND.

Sunday by the calendar—Sunday by the sweet Sabbath bells of the peaceful North, but what shall I name it here? Men are busy wrenching up and carrying away seats in a church near by, and leaving a clear area for a hospital; pallets for pews, the dead for the word of mercy. And why not? The worshipers that gathered there are scattered and gone. You may ask for the leaves of autumn as well. The old psalm has died out along the walls, and fancy halts at the thought of what may be heard in its stead.

Yesterday was gloomy with clouds and rain. To-day dawned out of Paradise. Would you have the picture? Stand with me as I stood this morning, near Major-General Granger's Headquarters, here in the heart of Chattanooga. As the sun comes up, the mists lift grandly, trail along the tops of the mountains, and are folded up in heaven. The horizon all around rises and falls like the waves of the sea. Stretching along the east and trending slightly away to the southwest, you see an undulating ridge edged with a thin fringe of trees. Along the sides, which have been shorn of their woods for the play of the battle-hammers, if you look closely, you shall see camps sprinkled like flocks away on till the ridge melts out of sight; you shall see guns and men in gray. That is Mission Ridge, and you are looking upon what your heart does not warm to. You are in the presence of the enemy.

Now, turning to the right, you look south upon the lowlands, and the farther edge of the picture is dotted with more tents and more men in gray. Away in the distance, a cone rises ambitiously, not far enough off to be blue, but you forget it in an instant as the eye climbs bravely up a wooded line, higher and higher, to a craggy crown, wrinkled with ravines, and crested with trees, that, hanging like a great frown between earth and heaven, then dropping abruptly away, as you turn southwestward, subsides into a valley through which the wandering Tennessee creeps into this Federal stronghold. Midway of the gigantic side, shorn of its oaks, like the Ridge, you see a house, a checker of white upon the brown swell of earth and stones. Lookout Mountain is before you, grim and grand. The glorious glimpses of five States granted to them who stand upon the mighty threshold between this world and that, are denied to us just now, and we must bide our time. You can look upon Tennessee, Georgia, Alabama; you can see the dim looming of the Blue Ridge and Bald Peak, and the smoky ranges of the "old North State," the shadow of whose King's Mountain is sacred for all time, since thence came that first whisper for independence which, at last, broke out aloud around the British throne. The morning has worn away to eight o'clock, when from the very tip of the crest rolls a little gray cloud, as if unseen hands were about to wind the rugged brow with a turban.

In an instant, a heavy growl and the rebel gun has said "good morning" to Hooker's camps in the Valley beyond. You cannot get out of sight of Lookout. Go where you will within all this horizon, yet, turning southward, there frowns the mountain. It rises like an everlasting thunder-storm that will never pass over. Satan might have offered the kingdoms of the world from that summit. Seen dimly through the mist, it looms up with its two thousand feet and recedes, but when the sun shines strongly out it draws so near as to startle you, and you feel as if you were beneath the eaves of a roof whence drips an iron rain. And yet, from the spot where we stand, it is three miles to its summit, three miles to Mission Ridge, and three miles to Moccasin Point.

But your eyes are not weary, and so they follow down the faltering line of Lookout, dip into the gateway of the Tennessee, and rise again to a red ridge, that seems to you, where you stand, like a vast tumulus big with the dead of an elder time. From it, even while you look, comes the Federal "good morning" back again. You hear the gun as it utters the shell, and then, traveling after it, the crash of the iron egg as it hatches on Lookout. That red ridge is Moccasin Point, whose sharp talk is a proverb. Glancing northward up the western horizon, is Raccoon Range, and

upon a peak of it, just opposite and west of us, is a
Federal signal-station.   Then away to the northwest
and across the north, the mountain-edges trace · the
· line of beauty, curving and blending until the graceful
profile of the horizon is complete.   But within this
sweep of grandeur lies a thing whose name shall endure
when yours and mine have been effaced by Time, like a
writing upon a slate by a wet finger—CHATTANOOGA.
Once a town with one main business street to give it a
little commercial pulsation ; residences, some of them
beautiful, a few of them stately, sprinkled all around
upon the acclivities, interspersed with more structures
built up in the true Southern architecture, holes in the
middle, or balconies, or the chimneys turned out of
doors.   A stinted, rusty-looking market-house subdued
beneath a chuckle-headed belfry, four or five churches
of indifferent fashion, two or three hotels whose entertainment has departed with the Boniface, and straggling tenements " of low degree " are pretty nearly all
that remain.   As you pass along the central street, the
dingy signs of old dead business catch the eye.   Where
" A. Baker, attorney-at-law," once uttered oracles and
tobacco-juice, Federal stores have taken Blackstone's
place ; where ribbons ran smoothly over the salesman's
fingers, boxes of hard-tack are piled, like Ossa and
Pelion come again.   Fences have gone lightly up in

camp-fires; tents are pitched like mushrooms in the flower-beds, trees have turned to ashes, shrubbery is trampled under foot, gardens are nothing better than mule-pens, shot and shell have left a token here and there, and, across the whole, War has scrawled his auto-graph. But never think you have seen the town at one glance; it is down here and up there and over yonder; the little hills swell beneath it like billows; you will gain the idea if I say it is a town gone to pieces in a heavy sea.

But a new architecture has sprung up;—slopes, val-leys, hills, as far as you can see, are covered with Federal camps. Smoky cones, grander wall-tents, nar-row streets of little stone and board kennels, chinked with mud like beavers' houses, snugly tucked into the hill-sides, and equipped with bits of fire-places that sometimes aspire to the dignity of marble, are every-where. It is nothing but camps, and then more camps. I wrote about "dead business," but I was too fast. It is *all* business, but conducted by the new firm of "U. S." The anvils ring, the stores are filled, wagons in endless lines and hurrying crowds throng all the streets, but the workman and the clerk is each a boy in blue. Chattanooga is as populous as an ant-hill. And there is more of the new architecture: breast-works, rifle-pits, forts, defenses of every name, crown

the slopes. Here, at your left elbow, is Fort Wood
that can talk to Mission Ridge : and there are Negley
and Palmer, and so on around the horizon. And then,
as if they had been poured out of the town like water,
spreading away to left and right and south, as you
stand facing Lookout, are Federal camps, drifting on
almost to the base of the Mountain, and lying bravely
beneath its grim shadow. The more you look, the
more you wonder how it can all be. It overturns your
notions of hostile armies, this neighborly nearness.
You see two thin picket-lines running parallel and a
few rods apart—not so far as you can jerk a peach-
stone. They pass lovingly together from your left,
down Mission Ridge, curve to the right along the lowlands and past the foot of the great mountain. They
are the line of blue and the line of gray.

And just there, in those lowlands, but sloping up the
side of Lookout, lies the mass of the enemy; then
curving away to the east and north it lines Mission
Ridge, thus presenting a crescent front five miles in
length, and throughout all we are snug up to them,
breast to breast. What effect do you think it would
have upon that hostile phase, to strike it near its northern horn and turn it back on Mission Ridge away from
its railroad communications, and strike it where it is
wedged into the foot of Lookout, thus doubling it
back upon itself ?

Signal-lights are features in celestial scenery that, like the jewels in the Southern Cross, never appear in your peaceful Northern skies. Now, had the reader who has stood beside me all the morning, been out with me upon the hills last night, he would have seen, just over the edge of the highest lift of Raccoon Range, a crazy planet, bigger than Venus at the full, waltzing after a mad fashion about another soberer light. But had he watched it for a while, he would have discovered there was "method in that madness" after all. The antic light describes a quadrant, makes a semi-circle, stops, rises, falls, sweeps right, sweeps left, rounds out an orbit, strikes off at a tangent. The Lieutenant of the Signal Corps is talking to somebody behind Lookout. Turning towards Mission Ridge, you would have seen lights of evil omen, for the hostile signals were working too; blazing, disappearing, showing here and there and yonder; now on the Mountain, now all along the Ridge, like wills-of-the-wisp. To-day the army telegraph gesticulates like Roscius, but it is flags and not lights that have gone crazy, and so the talk goes on around the sky.

At ten o'clock this morning, you were standing in front of Colonel Sherman's headquarters, and as you looked eastward you saw, without a glass, a column of the enemy moving slowly up the Ridge and a wagon-train creeping on after it. You took a glass and held the fellows as if by the button-hole. Just then a roar from Fort Wood, close above you, and a long, rushing, shivering cry quivers through the air; the shell crosses the intervals, strikes the Ridge at the heels of the lazy column, and its rate of motion is wonderfully accelerated. No steed was ever more obedient to the touch of the rowels. Again the "Rodman" speaks, and down comes the carriage of an angry gun for kindling-wood. It can toss its compliments as lightly over to Mission Ridge as you can toss an apple over the orchard fence. The shriek of a shell, if you have no musketry to soften it, is terrible, unearthly, the wail of a lost spirit. A solid shot has a soberer way with it, is attended by but one syllable of loud talk, plunges like a big beetle into the earth, and there's an end of it; while a shell, that does its duty, has thunder and a cloud at *both* ends of its line of flight. There goes Fort Wood again. Listen a few beats of the pulse, and yonder, well up the side of the Ridge, lies a fleece of smoke that was not there an instant ago, and here—*bomb*—comes the sound of the burning missile. A shell is a dissyllable.

And how about the rebel shells from Lookout, that drop now and then into town? Well, not much—at least not yet. Five minutes ago the gun flung a shell over the mountain's left shoulder, and growled at its brisk neighbor below, on Moccasin Point, or at our camps on its other side. It has, indeed, thrown shell beyond these Headquarters and struck a house, but they are plunging shots and the casualties have been few, unless a fragment, an ounce or so too heavy for your hat, may hit you on the head. They have generally exploded mid-air, and are regarded with perfect indifference by the boys. If one of them is laughing he finishes out the frolic; if he is a vicious Yankee, and whittling, he never looks up; if he is singing a stave of "Rally round the flag, boys," he does not. intermit a syllable but keeps right on. The unaffected indifference to this description of heavy rain would, I think, set you wondering. If Braxton Bragg, our neighbor over the way, is doing his best, and showing us all his teeth on Lookout, he needs a repetition of what old "Rough and Ready" *might* have said to his namesake, if not to him, a long time ago: "A little more grape, Captain Bragg!" But he has a fashion of sending a flag occasionally, with the injunction to remove non-combatants from the city, as he is going to shell. He sent such word again, a night or two ago, and word is pretty much all.

. We get direct news from "Dixie" daily. A Lieutenant and a couple of Sergeants came into our lines last night. The first-named, an intelligent young man,

stated that the army was making a grand move, though
he did not know its meaning, wherein he told us only
what we knew before, by the sight of the eyes. Another officer, belonging to a regiment in the front, came
across the neutral ground, the other day, and while
standing with our picket until he could be brought in,
actually heard them calling the roll of his company,
and when his name was reached, cried out, "here!"

THE SMITING OF THE SHIELD.

MONDAY—TWENTY-THIRD.

The battle has been given and won; the dear old
flag streams like a meteor from the craggy crown of
Lookout Mountain; Mission Ridge has been swept
with fire and steel as with a broom; the grim crescent
of the enemy, curving away along the range, from the
far northeast, south to the base of Lookout, has been
bent back upon itself and crushed like a buzzard's egg;
the terrible arc of iron, five miles long, that bent like a
quadrant around half of our horizon, is broken and
scattered; the key has at last been turned in the Chattanooga lock; the enemy must fly from East Tennessee, like shadows before the morning; the Nashville
and Chattanooga Railroad is once more true to its
name; the Tennessee River is all clear to its landing;

our communications are perfected and confirmed, and
to the Federal army Chattanooga is no longer the end,
but the beginning of things; the step put forward is
not to be withdrawn; our eyes may now be lifted and
look beyond Chattanooga. Thanks be to GOD and the
Boys in Blue!

I sit down utterly unequal to a task in which pride
and grief are strangely blended; and yet, in an instant,
a half-cheer, exultant, triumphant, comes to my lip,
and to-night, under this cloudless sky, the way swept
clean to Heaven for our boys going there, I turn to the
painted emblem that blossomed so strangely upon
Lookout at break of day, a thousand times more dear
for their dear sake who died, and say: Oh, Flag,
that would make us bankrupt but that thy folds are
priceless!

Last Friday morning, at daylight, the battle was to
begin. Sherman's splendid columns, moving on from
Bridgeport through Shell Mound and Whiteside among
the hills to Brown's Ferry, crossing in the night; then
on the north side of the Tennessee to the mouth of
Cilico Creek, and there, bridging the river, and having
taken position upon our extreme left, five miles to the
northeast, were to attain Mission Ridge and roll the
enemy before them. At the same moment, Hooker,
whose camps lay along the western side of the moun-

tain, at our extreme right, was to make a demonstration upon Lookout, with a portion of the Twelfth Army Corps and a Division of the Fourth; Granger was to swing round toward Rossville, with the Fourteenth Corps at his right; and Johnson, commanding Rousseau's old Division of the Fourteenth Corps, and Howard's command of the Eleventh, were to hold the town and act as reserves. Thus, our completed line, reading, English fashion, from left to right, by corps, would be Generals Sherman, Howard, Granger, Palmer, Hooker.

But a heavy rain setting in, the terrible roads were rendered almost impassable, and Sherman, with his ponderous trains of artillery, struggled on; but Friday, Saturday, Sunday, and Monday, came and went, and his journey was undone. General Grant, with his sterling sense, had ordered a body of cavalry to remove every resident, whether friend or foe—General Grant very wisely taking nothing for granted—from Sherman's route, that no tidings of his precise destination might reach the enemy. But the delay, at once so unavoidable and lamented, marred a plan that was masterly, being nothing less than to strike at the same hour the two horns of the lurid crescent and double it back upon itself. It was, indeed, a gigantic piece of mechanism, but the rain came, rusted, if I may say so, the wheels on their axles, and the mechanism was motionless.

What a strange problem is a battle, dependent, sometimes, upon a breath of wind or a drop of water!

Meanwhile it was apparent that the enemy apprehended coming danger, for on Sunday morning two
divisions moved northward along Mission Ridge and
took position on his extreme right. All that beautiful
Sunday, the rebel lines were restless; trains were moving, brigades passing and repassing, like the sliding pictures in a camera obscura; there was "a fearful looking
for" of coming judgment. All that beautiful Sunday
there was anxious expectation in Chattanooga; field-
glasses were everywhere sweeping the mountains; I
walked through the camps and the boys were a shade
less merry than is their wont; the hush of the coming
storm was in the air. And so the Sabbath wore away.
Then Federal signals flashed from hill to hill along the
west, like "the writing on the wall," and through the
dusk Howard's columns moved like deeper shadows
across the town. All night long I heard the tramp of
the men and the hollow rumbling of artillery, and as
the moon came up, the sentinels looked down upon it
all, like sentries from a tower. Deserters, both officers
and men, came into our picket lines that night; the
enemy was astir; rations had been issued; baggage
sent to the rear; they were making ready for business.
Monday, cloudy and dull, dragged through its morning.

Let me show you a landscape that shall not fade out from "the lidless eye of time" long after we are all dead. A half-mile from the eastern border of Chattanooga is a long swell of land sparsely sprinkled with houses, flecked thickly with tents, and checkered with two or three grave-yards. On its summit stand the red earthworks of Fort Wood, with its great guns frowning from the angles. Mounting the parapet and facing eastward you have a singular panorama. Away to your left is a shining elbow of the Tennessee, a lowland of woods, a long-drawn valley, glimpses of houses. At your right you have wooded undulations with clear intervals extending down and around to the valley at the eastern base of Lookout. From the Fort the smooth ground descends rapidly to a little plain, a sort of trough in the sea, then a fringe of oak woods, then an acclivity, sinking down to a second fringe of woods, until full in front of you and three-fourths of a mile distant, rises Orchard Knob, a conical mound, perhaps an hundred feet high, once wooded, but now bald. Then ledges of rocks and narrow breadths of timber, and rolling sweeps of open ground, for two miles more, until the whole rough and stormy landscape seems to dash against Mission Ridge, three miles distant, that lifts like a sea-wall eight hundred feet high, wooded, rocky, precipitous, wrinkled with ravines. This is, in

truth, the grand feature of the scene, for it extends
north as far as you can see, with fields here and there
cut down through the woods to the ground, and lying
on the hillsides like brown linen to bleach; and you
feel, as you look at them, as if they are in danger of
slipping down the Ridge into the road at its base.
And then it curves to the southwest, just leaving you
a way out between it and Lookout Mountain. · Altogether the rough, furrowed landscape looks as if the
Titans had plowed and forgotten to harrow it.   The
thinly fringed summit of the Ridge varies in width
from twenty to fifty feet, and houses looking like cigar-
boxes are dotted along it.   On the top of that wall are
rebels and batteries; below the first pitch, three hundred feet down, are more rebels and batteries, and still
below are their camps and rifle-pits, sweeping five miles.
At your right, and in the rear, is Fort Negley, the old
"Star" Fort of Confederate *regime;* its next neighbor
is Fort King, under the frown of Lookout; yet to the
right is the battery of Moccasin Point.   Finish out the
picture on either hand with Federal earthworks and
saucy angles, fancy the embankment of the Charleston
and Memphis Railroad drawn diagonally, like an awk-
ward score, across the plain far at your feet, and I think
you have the tremendous Theatre, and now what next,
if not, in Hamlet's words, "the play's the thing!"

The Federal forces lay along the ridgy slope to the right and left of Fort Wood; the enemy's advance held Orchard Knob in force, and their breastworks and rifle-pits seamed the landscape. At half-past twelve o'clock, Major-General Granger received an order to make a reconnoissance in force towards the base of Mission Ridge, and feel the enemy, supposed to be massing in our immediate front and on Lookout Mountain. It was a strange scene. There was to be no more use for the two lines of pickets that for so many days and nights had stood in friendly neighborhood, exchanged the jest and the daily news, and sat at each other's fires. Ours were to be recalled; theirs were to be thrust back, and the thin veneering of battle's double front rudely torn away. At half-past twelve the order came; at one, two divisions of the Fourth Corps made ready to move; at ten minutes before two, twenty-five thousand Federal troops were in line of battle. The line of skirmishers moved lightly out, and swept true as a sword-blade into the edge of the field. You should have seen that splendid line, two miles long, as straight and unwavering as a ray of light. On they went, driving in the pickets before them; shots of musketry, like the first great drops of summer rain upon a roof, pattered along the line. One fell here, another there, but still like joyous heralds before a royal progress, the skirmishers passed on. From wood and rifle-pit, from rocky ledge and mountain-top, sixty-five thousand rebels watched these couriers bearing the gift of battle in their hands. The bugle sounded from Fort Wood, and the divisions of Wood and Sheridan began to move; the latter, out from the right, threatened a heavy attack; the former, forth from the left, dashed on into the rough road of the battle. Black rifle-pits were tipped with fire; sheets of flame flashed out of the woods; the spatter of musketry deepened into volleys and rolled like muffled drums; hostile batteries opened from the ledges; the "Rodmans" joined in from Fort Wood; bursting shell and gusts of shrapnel filled the air; the echoes roused up and growled back from the mountains, the rattle was a roar, and yet those gallant fellows moved steadily on; down the slope, through the wood, up the hills, straight for Orchard Knob as the crow flies, moved that glorious wall of blue.

The air grew dense and blue; the gray clouds of smoke surged up the sides of the valley. It was a terrible journey they were making, those men of ours; and three-fourths of a mile in sixty minutes was splendid progress. They neared the Knob; the enemy's fire converged; the arc of batteries poured in upon them lines of fire, like the rays they call a "glory" about the

head of Madonna and the Child, but they went up the
rugged altar of Orchard Knob at the double-quick with
a cheer; they wrapped, like a cloak, round an Alabama
regiment that defended it, and swept them down on
our side of the mound.   Prisoners had begun to come
in before; they streamed across the field like files of
geese.   Then on for a second altar, Brush Knob—nearly
a half-mile to the northeast—and bristling with a battery; it was swept of foes and garnished with Federal
blue in thirty minutes.

The Third Division of the Fourth Corps had made
a splendid march; they had bent our line outward to
the enemy like Apollo's bow, and so Howard at
Wood's right, and Sheridan at his left, swung out to
cut new swaths and leave the edges even, as we went
right through this harvest-field of splendid valor and
heroic death.   At four o'clock, Granger's headquarters
were on Orchard Knob, and the cruel storm beat on.
On the left, fronting the section of the Eleventh Corps
led by General Schurz, was a range of rifle-pits whence
the stubborn enemy were not driven, and the General,
whose quick eye nothing on that broad field escaped,
ordered two brisk twelve-pound Parrotts of Bridges'
Battery, planted upon Orchard Knob, to give them an
enfilading fire where, on his left, the ends of their rifle-
pits showed in the edge of the wood like the mouth of

a wolf's burrow. You should have seen that motley crew climb out as the splendid fire swept through, and scurry out of sight. It was their ditch, indeed, but they were not quite ready to die in it. The left of the Federal line not advancing to occupy the work, its old tenants crept back one by one, and lay snug as ever. Thrice did Granger sweep the rifle-pits, and General Beattie was ordered round with three regiments to re-enforce the left, and the line came squarely up.

At four o'clock the gallant Hazen, at the head of his brigade, charged the rifle-pits at the right of Orchard Knob, up the hill, carried them at the point of the bayonet, and swooped up three hundred prisoners. Here Major Buck of the 93d Ohio fell mortally wounded, and the 93d and 124th Ohio lost thirty killed and one hundred wounded. While the terrible play was going on here, there was neither silence nor inactivity there. Moccasin Point thundered at the camps in the valley at the south, and Lookout growled at the Point, Fort King uttered a word on its own account, and Wood laid its shells about where it pleased, their little rolls of smoke lying on the Ridge like fleeces of wool.

If you have glance or thought for anything but the grand action of the drama, you can see the signals fluttering like white wings from Fort Wood, from away to the left of the line, from the brow of Orchard Knob, from the left of Raccoon Range across the town. On the summit of Mission Ridge, a little to the southeast of Fort Wood, is a cluster of buildings; a glass will bring them so near that you can discern the gray horse ready saddled at the door. You are looking upon the headquarters of Braxton Bragg. All these hours, he has been watching the impetuous surge of Federal gallantry that swept his smoky legions out of their rifle-pits, off from their vantage-ground, over the swells, through the selvedge of woods, into their rifle-pits and behind their defenses.

Listening with his heart to all the tumult of that terrible afternoon, no man can tell how three little figures can truthfully express the Federal loss, but he must believe and be glad when I tell him that "420" are those figures. The enemy must keep counting on to seven hundred before his bloody roll is called.

Of the heroic coolness of our army, how can I say enough? Moving against thirty thousand men, possessing every advantage of position, defenses, numbers engaged—everything, indeed, but having chosen a day of battle—all men will take up the words of General Howard, and pass them round the land: "I knew that Western men would fight well, but I did *not* know that they went into battle and stormed strong works like

men on dress parade!" And will the Illinois reader
who has faithfully borne me company look over the
regiments that compose that splendid corps — the
Fourth—and see how many of them belong to him.
All through the brigades of Beattie and Willich, Hazen
and Wagner, Harkner and Colonel Sherman, he will find
something from the Prairie State that will make true
over and over the name that has passed from a perished
race of kings, and set, like the seal of the covenant
forever, upon a broad realm, now in these battle years,
to be worn once more by them that dwell therein—
ILLINI—we are MEN!

The battle ends with the ended day, the commanding General is in the center of his new front far out in
the field; the pickets assume their old proximity in a
new neighborhood; no musket-shot startles the silence,
and behind the fresh breastworks that have carried the
heavy labors of soul and sinew far on into the night,
the Federal forces sleep upon their arms; to dream,
perchance, of fierce assault and sweeping triumph; to
wake, perhaps, to a half-reluctant sense of another
heavy day of struggle and of blood, for the threshold
of approach is only swept, and there before them
waits the enemy.

THE CAPTURE OF LOOKOUT MOUNTAIN.

TUESDAY—TWENTY-FOURTH.

I am looking down upon three boys that lie side by side on the ground. Three bits of twine bind those willing feet of theirs, that shall never again move at "the double-quick" to the charge. They were among the heroes of Lookout Mountain. They were killed yesterday. And to-day—let me think what *is* to-day. Away there at the North, there were song and sermon; and the old family table, that had been drooping in the corner, spread its wide wings; and the children came flocking home "like doves to their windows;" and the threshold made music to their feet—alas, for the three pairs beside me!—and the welcome went round the bright hearth. It is THANKSGIVING to-day! Let the mothers give thanks, if they can, for the far-away feet that grew beautiful as they hastened to duty and halted in death. Even while the heart of the loyal land was lifted in a psalm for the blessings it had numbered, *another* was winging its way northward—the tidings of triumph from the mountains of the Cumberland!

Tuesday broke cold and cheerless; it was a Scottish morning, and the air was dim with mist. I crossed the ground over which our boys had marched so grandly on

Monday afternoon, down into the valley of death and
glory, where they had lain all night in line of battle.
Brave hearts! They were ready and eager for a second
day's journey; they had put their hands to the burning
plowshare, and there was no thought of looking back.
Beyond them lay the hostile camps, and Mission Ridge
with its three furrows of rifle-pits, and the enemy
swarming like gray ants on the hills. You would have
wondered, as I did, at the formidable line of defense
the boys had thrown up when they came to a halt, and
the terrible music they marched to had died out with
the day. Rocks and logs had been piled in great windrows, filled in with earth, and could have withstood a
stout assault. There had been a great deal of sneering
among the Generals who "shoulder the *pen* and show
how fields are won," about fighting with shovels. The
man fit to command no more forgets the pickaxe than
he forgets the powder. The Fourth Corps is remarkable for "making ready" before it takes aim, and among
the Generals I may name Sheridan, as a man who never
marches without the tools and never halts without
intrenching. *Semper paratus*—always prepared—is the
motto. Such men, it is, among the Federal chiefs, that
give the following little colloquy its point: After the
battle of Chicamauga, General Johnston of Mississippi,
thus accosted Bragg: " Having beaten the enemy,

why didn't you pursue the advantage?" "Well," replied Bragg, "my losses were heavy, you see, and my line was pretty long, and by the time I could get under motion the —— Yankees would have been *ten* feet *under ground!*"

A splendid compliment, look at it in any way you please, and competent testimony to the wisdom of numbering pickaxe and shovel among weapons of war.

But reader and writer were out together along the lines in the gray of the morning. Our wicked little battery on Orchard Knob had "ceased from troubling;" Fort Wood was dumb, and not a voice from the "Parrott" perches anywhere. Stray ambulances—those flying hospitals—were making their way back to the town, and soldiers were digging graves on the hill-sides. Interrogation points glittered in men's eyes as they turned an ear to the northeast and listened for Sherman. By and by a little fleet of soldier-laden pontoon boats came drifting down the river, and I hastened to meet them as they landed. The boys in high feather tumbled out, the inevitable coffee-kettle swinging from their bayonets. If a Federal soldier should be fellow-traveler with Bunyan's Pilgrim, I almost believe that tin kettle of his would be heard tinkling after him to the very threshold of the "Gate Beautiful." "Well, boys—what now?" "We've put down the pontoon—

taken nineteen rebel pickets without firing a gun—run
the rebel blockade—drawn a shot—nobody hurt—Sherman's column is half over—bully for Sherman!" Those
fellows had been thirty hours without rest, and were as
fresh-hearted and dashing as so many thorough-breds.
They had wrought all night long with their lives in
their hands, and not a trace of hardship or a breath of
complaining.   The heavy drudgery of army life, without which campaigns could never bear the red blossom
of battle, seldom, I fancy, elicits the thanks of commanding Generals.

Perhaps it was eleven o'clock on Tuesday morning,
when the rumble of artillery came in gusts from the
valley to the west of Lookout. Climbing Signal Hill,
I could see volumes of smoke rolling to and fro, like
clouds from a boiling caldron. The mad surges of
tumult lashed the hill till they cried aloud, and roared
through the gorges till you might have fancied all the
thunders of a long summer tumbled into that valley
together. And yet the battle was unseen. It was like
hearing voices from the under-world. Meanwhile it
began to rain; skirts of mist trailed over the woods
and swept down the ravines, but our men trusted in
Providence, kept their powder dry, and played on. It
was the second day of the drama; it was the second act
I was hearing; it was the touch on the enemy's left.

The assault upon Lookout had begun! Glancing at the mighty crest crowned with a precipice, and now hung round about, three hundred feet down, with a curtain of clouds, my heart misgave me. It could never be taken.

But let me step aside just here from the simple story of what I saw, to detail, as concisely as I can, Hooker's admirable design. His force consisted of two brigades of the Fourth Corps, under the command of General Cruft, General Whittaker's and Colonel Grose's—having in them five Illinois regiments, the 59th, 75th, 84th, 96th, and 115th; the First Division of the Twelfth Corps under General Geary, and Osterhaus in reserve. It was a formidable business they had in hand: to carry a mountain and scale a precipice near two thousand feet high, in the teeth of a battery and the face of two intrenched brigades. Hooker ordered Cruft to move directly south along the western base of the mountain, while he would remain in the valley close under Lookout, and make a grand demonstration with small-arms and artillery. The enemy, roused out by all this "sound and fury," were to come forth from their camps and works, high up the western side of the mountain, and descend to dispute Hooker's noisy passage; Cruft, when the roar behind him deepened into "confusion worse confounded," was to turn upon his heel, move obliquely up the mountain upon the enemy's camps, in the enemy's rear, wheel round the monster, and up to the white house I have already described, and take care of himself while he took Lookout.

Hooker thundered and the enemy came down like the Assyrian, while Whittaker on the right, and Colonel Ireland of Geary's command on the left, having moved out from Wauhatchie, some five miles from the mountain, at five in the morning, pushed up to Chattanooga Creek, threw over it a bridge, made for Lookout Point, and there formed the right under the shelf of the mountain, the left resting on the creek. And then the play began; the enemy's camps were seized, his pickets surprised and captured, the strong works on the Point taken, and the Federal front moved on. Charging upon him, they leaped over his works as the wicked twin Roman leaped over his brother's mud-wall, the 40th Ohio capturing his artillery and taking a Mississippi regiment, and gained the white house. And there they stood, 'twixt heaven and—Chattanooga. But above them, grand and sullen, lifted the precipice; and they were men and not eagles. The way was strown with natural fortifications, and from behind rocks and trees they delivered their fire, contesting inch by inch the upward way. The sound of the battle rose and fell; now fiercely renewed, and now dying away. And

Hooker thundered on in the valley, and the echoes of his howitzers bounded about the mountains like volleys of musketry. That curtain of cloud was hung around the mountain by the GOD of battles—even our GOD. It was the veil of the temple that could not be rent. A captured Colonel declared that had the day been clear, their sharpshooters would have riddled our advance like pigeons, and left the command without a leader, but friend and foe were wrapped in a seamless mantle, and two hundred will cover the entire Federal loss, while our brave mountaineers strewed Lookout with four hundred dead, and captured a thousand prisoners.

Our entire forces bore themselves bravely; not a straggler in the command, they all came splendidly up to the work, and the whole affair was graced with signal instances of personal valor. Lieutenant Smith, of the 40th Ohio, leaped over the works, discharged his revolver six times like the ticking of a clock, seized a sturdy foe by the hair, and gave him the heel of the "Colt" over the head. Colonel Ireland was slightly wounded, and Major Acton, of the 40th Ohio, was shot through the heart while leading a bayonet charge.

And now returning to my point of observation, I was waiting in painful suspense to see what should come out of the roaring caldron in the valley, now and then,

I confess, casting an eye up to the big gun of Lookout, lest it might toss something my way, over its left
shoulder, I, a non-combatant and bearing no arms but
a Faber's pencil, "Number 2," when something was *born*
out of the mist—I cannot better convey the idea—
and appeared on the shorn side of the mountain, below
and to the west of the white house. It was the head
of the Federal column! And there it held, as if
it were riveted to the rock, and the line of blue, a half
mile long, swung slowly around from the left like the
index of a mighty dial, and swept up the brown face of
the mountain. The bugles of this city of camps were
sounding high noon, when in two parallel columns the
troops moved up the mountain, in the rear of the
enemy's rifle-pits, which they swept at every fire. Ah,
I wish you had been here. It needed no glass to see
it; it was only just beyond your hand. And there, in
the center of the columns, fluttered the blessed flag.
"My God! what flag is that?" men cried. And up
steadily it moved. I could think of nothing but a
gallant ship-of-the-line grandly lifting upon the great
billows and riding out the storm. It was a scene never
to fade out. Pride and pain struggled in my heart for
the mastery, but faith carried the day: I believed in
the flag and took courage. Volleys of musketry and
crashes of cannon, and then those lulls in a battle even

more terrible than the tempest. At four o'clock an aid came straight down the mountain into the city; the first Federal by that route in many a day. Their ammunition ran low—they wanted powder upon the mountain! He had been two hours descending, and how much longer the return!

Night was closing rapidly in, and the scene was growing sublime. The battery at Moccasin Point was sweeping the road to the mountain. The brave little fort at its left was playing like a heart in a fever. The cannon upon the top of Lookout were pounding away at their lowest depression. The flash of the guns fairly *burned* through the clouds; there was an instant of silence, here, there, yonder, and the tardy thunder leaped out after the swift light. For the first time, perhaps, since that mountain began to burn beneath the gold and crimson sandals of the sun, it was in eclipse. The cloud of the summit and the smoke of the battle had met half-way and mingled. Here was Chattanooga, but Lookout had vanished! It was Sinai over again with its thunderings and lightnings and thick darkness, and the LORD was on our side. Then the storm ceased, and occasional dropping shots told off the evening till half-past nine, and then a crashing volley and a rebel yell and a desperate charge. It was their good-night to our boys; good night to the moun-

tain.   They had been met on their own vantage
ground; they had been driven one and a half miles.
The Federal foot touched the hill, indeed, but above
still towered the precipice.

At ten o'clock, a growing line of lights glittered
obliquely across the breast of Lookout.   It made our
eyes dim to see it.   It was the Federal autograph
scored along the mountain.   They were our camp-fires.
Our wounded lay there all the dreary night of rain,
unrepining and content.   Our unharmed heroes lay
there upon their arms.   Our dead lay there, "and
surely they slept well."   At dawn, Captain Wilson and
fifteen men of the 8th Kentucky crept up among the
rocky clefts, handing their guns one to another—"like
them that gather samphire — dreadful trade!"—and
stood at length upon the summit.   The entire regiment
pushed up after them, formed in line, threw out
skirmishers and advanced five miles to Summerton.
Artillery and infantry had all fled in the night, nor left
a wreck behind.   The plan was opening as beautifully
as a flower.   General Sherman's apprehended approach
upon the other extremity of the line had set the
enemy's front all dressing to the right.   Hardee, of
"Tactics" memory, who had been upon the mountain,
moved round the line on Sunday, leaving two brigades
and the attraction of gravitation—to wit, the precipice

—to hold the left, yet farther depleted by the splendid march already made upon the enemy's center
Then GOD let down a fold of his pavilion, our men
were heroes and the work was done. The capture
afforded inexpressible relief to the army. There the
enemy had looked down defiant, sentries pacing our
very walls. Every angle of a Federal work, every gun,
every new disposition of a regiment, was as legible as
a page of an open book. You can never quite know
how beautiful was that cordon of lights flung like a
royal order across the breast of the mountain.

One thing more, and all I shall try to give you of the
stirring story will have been told. Just as the sun was
touching up the old Department of the Cumberland,
that Captain Wilson and his fifteen men, near where
the gun had crouched and growled at all the land,
waved the regimental flag, in sight of Tennessee, Alabama, Georgia, the old 'North State" and South
Carolina—waved it there, and the right of the Federal
front, lying far beneath, caught a glimpse of its flutter,
and a cheer rose to the top of the mountain, and ran
from regiment to regiment through whole brigades and
broad divisions, till the boys away round in the face of
Mission Ridge passed it along the line of battle. "The
sight of the gridiron did my soul good," said General
Meigs. 'What is it? Our flag? Did I help put it

there?" murmured a poor wounded fellow, and died without the sight.

> Oh, glimpse of clear heaven,
>   Artillery riven !
> The Fathers' old fallow GOD seeded with Stars—
>   Thy furrows were turning
>   When plowshares were burning,
> And the half of each "bout" is redder than Mars !

>   Flaunt forever thy story,
>   Oh, wardrobe of glory !
> Where the Fathers laid down their mantles of blue,
>   And challenged the ages,
>   —Oh, grandest of gages !—
> In covenant solemn, eternal and true !

>   Oh, Flag glory-rifted !
>   To-day thunder-drifted,
> Like a flower of strange grace upon LOOKOUT's grim surge,
>   On some Federal fold
>   A new tale shall be told,
> And the record immortal emblazon thy verge !

And so at Wednesday's dawn, ended the second act of the drama of Mission Ridge—Wednesday whose sun should set upon the third, the grandest and the last.

THE STORMING OF MISSION RIDGE.

WEDNESDAY—TWENTY-FIFTH.

The stars and stripes floated from Lookout on Wednesday at sunrise. At twelve on that day, something with the cry of a loon was making its way up the river. Screaming through the mountains, it emerged at last into Chattanooga, and its looks were a match for its lungs—an ugly little craft more like a backwoods cabin adrift than a steamer, it was the sweetest-voiced and prettiest piece of naval architecture that ever floated upon the Tennessee. The flag on the crest and the boat on the stream were parts of the same story: first, the fight on the mountain; then, the boat on the river. Never did result crowd more closely on the heels of action. When the thunder began to roll around Lookout, the boys in line before Mission Ridge cried out: "Old Hooker is opening the cracker line!" And when the next noon they heard the shriek of the steamer, they laughingly said, "The cracker line is opened!" and went straight into the fight with a will. They have a direct way of "putting things" in the army.

I do not think that going about Chattanooga, last Wednesday morning, you would have discerned an

impending battle.   The current of regular business was
not checked; the play of men's little passions was as
lively as ever.   Jest and laughter eddied round the
street corners, and pepper-and-salt groups of children
frolicked in sunny places.   But there *were* signs of
heavy weather.   The doors of the ordnance depots
swung open, the sentinels stood aside, and ammunition
was passing out.   You could see "canvas-backed"
wagons working their way out of town to the eastward, apparently but little in them, and yet laboring
beneath their freight.   Grape and canister and shot
and shell make heavy loads as well as heavy hearts.
A building here and there is cleared and strangely
furnished with long rows of pallets.   Ambulances set
forth, one after another; they are all going one way;
they are bound for the valley of Mission Ridge.   And
if all this should fail to set you thinking, yet there are
things that may, perhaps, disturb the steady stroke of
an easy-going heart.   Sitting with me, last Tuesday
night, you would have heard such talk as this.   A
chief-of-staff is speaking: "Jemmy, here is a package
of money I'll leave with you till I come back."   "Lend
me your watch," said a dashing young Major to a
comrade, "and here's a hundred dollars if I should
forget to return it to-morrow night, you know,' and
the officer swallowed a little memory of something and

went out.   You part the folds of tent after tent;
writing letters here, burning letters there, getting ready
for the longest of all journeys that yet can be made in
a minute.   "Well," said an officer that night, "I shall
be in the hottest place in the field to-morrow, but do
you know?—the bullet is not run that will kill me,"
and the gallant fellow dropped off into a child-like
sleep, while I lay awake and was troubled.   And he
told the truth—the bullet was *not* moulded—for a little
after four the next afternoon, a bursting shell carried
away the "pound of flesh" that Shylock craved, and
again he fell asleep, in the arms of the All-Father.
Good night!

If seeing for one's self is an art, seeing for another is
a mystery, requiring, I mistrust, a better pair of eyes
than mine.   But if my readers will accept a straight-
forward, simple story of what one man saw of Wednesday's work, as bare of embellishment as the bayonets
that glittered to the charge, here it is.   You are standing again on Orchard Knob, the center of our line of
advance; Mission Ridge is before; Fort Wood behind;
the shining elbow of the Tennessee to the left; Lookout to the right.   Never was theatre more magnificent.
Never was drama worthier of such surroundings.

The same grand heroic line of battle, but a little
longer and stronger, silently stretches away on either

hand. Breaking it up into syllables and reading from left to right, you have Howard's Eleventh Corps; Baird's division of the Fourteenth Corps, with the brigades of Turchin, Vandevere, and Croxton; Wood's division of the Fourth Corps, with the brigades of Beattie, Willich and Hazen; Sheridan's division, with the brigades of Wagner, Sherman and Harker; King's brigade of regulars, and Johnson's division of the Fourteenth Corps. And then, at the tips of the wings, on farthest left and right, are Sherman and Hooker. That portion of the line distinct from where you stand —how rich the homes of Illinois have made it! The 24th, 104th—and yonder the old, dashing 19th—the 25th, 33d, 89th, 100th, 22d, 27th, 42d, 51st, 79th, 36th, 88th, 74th, 44th, and 73d—each with its tale of battle, its roll of honor and its glorious dead—how glows the glittering line! Illinois was on Lookout yesterday; Illinois is over there with Sherman to-day. GOD bless the mother—GOD save the sons!

Imagine a chain of Federal forts, built in between with walls of living men, the line flung northward out of sight, and southward beyond Lookout. Imagine a chain of mountains crowned with batteries and manned with hostile troops through a six-mile sweep, set over against us in plain sight, and you have the two fronts— the blue, the gray. Imagine the center of our line

pushed out a mile and a half towards Mission Ridge—
the boss, a full mile broad, of a mighty shield—and
you have the situation as it was on Wednesday
morning, at sunrise.

The iron heart of Sherman's column began to be
audible, like the fall of great trees in the depth of the
forest, as it beat beyond the woods on the extreme left.
Over roads indescribable, and conquering lions of difficulties that met him all the way, he had at length
arrived with his command of the Army of the Tennessee. The roar of his guns was like the striking of
a great clock, and grew nearer and louder, as the morning wore away. Along the center all was still. Our
men lay, as they had lain since Tuesday night, motionless behind the works. Generals Grant, Thomas, Granger, Meigs, Hunter, Reynolds, were grouped at Orchard
Knob, here; Bragg, Breckenridge, Hardee, Stevens,
Cleburn, Bates, Walker, were waiting on Mission Ridge,
yonder. And Sherman's Northern clock tolled on! At
noon, a pair of steamers, screaming in the river across
the town, telling over, in their own wild way, our mountain triumph on the right, strangely pierced the hushed
breath of air between the two lines of battle with a
note or two of the music of peaceful life.

At one o'clock, the signal-flag at Fort Wood was
a-flutter. Scanning the horizon, another flag, glancing

like a lady's handkerchief, showed white across a field
lying high and dry upon the ridge three miles to the
northeast, and answered back. The center and Sherman's corps had spoken. As the hour went by, all
semblance to falling tree and tolling clock had vanished; it was a rattling roar; the ring of Sherman's
iron knuckles knocking at the northern door of Mission
Ridge for entrance. Moving nearer the river, I could
see the breath of Sherman's panting artillery, and the
fiery gust from the enemy's guns on Tunnel Hill, the
point of Mission Ridge. They had massed there the
corps of Hardee and Buckner, as upon a battlement,
utterly inaccessible, save by one steep, narrow way,
commanded by their guns. A thousand men could
hold it against a host. And right in front of this bold
abutment of the Ridge, is that broad, clear field,
skirted by woods. Across this tremendous threshold
up to death's door, moved Sherman's column. Twice
it advanced, and twice I saw it swept back in bleeding
lines before the furnace-blast, until that russet field
seemed some strange page ruled thick with blue and
red. Bright valor was in vain; they lacked the ground
to stand on; they wanted, like the giant of old story, a
touch of earth to make them strong. It was the devil's
own corner. Before them was a lane, whose upper end
the rebel cannon swallowed. Moving by the right

flank or the left flank, nature opposed them with precipitous heights. There was nothing for it but straight
across the field swept by an enfilading fire, and up to
the lane down which drove the storm. They could
unfold no broad front, and so the losses were less than
seven hundred, that must otherwise have swelled to
thousands. The musketry fire was delivered with terrible emphasis; two dwellings, in one of which Federal
wounded were lying, set on fire by the enemy, began to
send up tall columns of smoke, streaked red with
flame; the grand and the terrible were blended.

If Sherman did not roll the enemy along the Ridge
like a carpet, at least he rendered splendid service, for
he held a huge ganglion of the foe as firmly on their
right as if he had them in the vice of the "lame Lem-
nian" who forged the thunder-bolts. And Illinois was
there, too, with her veterans. Under General M. L.
Smith there were the 55th, 116th and 127th; the 26th,
40th, 48th, 90th and 103d led on by General Ewing; in
the Seventeenth Corps, the 56th, 63d, and 93d, under
General John E. Smith; the 82d in the Eleventh, under
Schurz; General J. C. Davis, of the Fourteenth, commanded the 10th, 16th, 60th, 78th, 85th, 86th, 101st,
110th, 125th, and 34th. Such was the magnificent
material from the Army of the Tennessee; but I thank
GOD that not a tithe could be called into action; the

day was won without it. General Corse's, Colonel
Jones' and Colonel Loomis' brigades led the way, and
were drenched with blood. Here, Colonel O'Meara, of
the 90th Illinois, fell; here, its Lieutenant-Colonel,
Stuart, received a fearful wound. Here, its brave
young Captains knelt at the crimson shrine, and never
rose from worshiping. Here, one hundred and sixty
of its three hundred and seventy heroes were beaten
with the bloody rain. The brigades of Generals
Mathias and Smith came gallantly up to the work.
Fairly blown out of the enemy's guns, and scorched
with flame, they were swept down the hill only to
stand fast for a new assault. Let no man dare to say
they did not acquit themselves well and nobly. To
living and dead in the commands of Sherman and
Howard who struck a blow that day—out of my heart
I utter it—hail and farewell! And as I think it all
over, glancing again along that grand heroic line of the
Federal Epic—I commit the story with a child-like
faith to History, sure that when she gives her clear,
calm record of that day's famous work, standing like
Ruth among the reapers in the fields that feed the
world, she will declare the grandest staple of the
Northwest is MAN!

The brief November afternoon was half gone; it was
yet thundering on the left; along the center all was

still. At that very hour, Whittaker and Grose, under
the immediate command of General Crufts, were making a fierce assault upon the enemy's left near Rossville, four miles down towards the old field of Chicamauga. They carried the Ridge; Mission Ridge seems
everywhere; they strewed its summit with the dead;
they held it, the 51st Ohio, Lieutenant-Colonel Wood,
playing a part of which the "Old Guard" in the little
Corsican's palmy days might well be proud. And thus
the tips of the Federal army's wide-spread wings
flapped grandly. But it had not swooped; the gray
quarry yet perched upon Mission Ridge; the hostile
army was terribly battered at the edges, but there full
in our front it grimly waited, biding out its time. If
the horns of the crescent could not be doubled crush-
ingly together in a shapeless mass, possibly it might be
sundered at its center and tumbled in fragments over
the other side of Mission Ridge. Sherman was hammering upon the left; Hooker was holding hard in
Chattanooga Valley; the Fourth Corps, that rounded
out our center, grew impatient of restraint; the day
was waning; but little time remained to complete the
commanding General's grand design; his hour had
come; his work was full before him.

And what a work that was, to make a weak man
falter and a brave man think! One and a half miles

to traverse, with narrow fringes of woods, rough valleys, sweeps of open fields, rocky acclivities, to the
base of the Ridge, and no foot in all the breadth
withdrawn from rebel sight; no foot that could not be
played upon by rebel cannon, like a piano's keys,
under Thalberg's stormy fingers. The base attained,
what then? A heavy work, packed with the enemy,
rimming it like a battlement. That work carried, and
what then? A hill struggling up out of the valley four
hundred feet, rained on by bullets, swept by shot and
shell; another line of works and then, up like a Gothic
roof, rough with rocks, a-wreck with fallen trees, four
hundred more; another ring of fire and iron, and then
the crest and then the enemy.

To dream of such a journey would be madness; to
devise it a thing incredible; to do it a deed impossible.
But Grant was guilty of them all, and was equal to the
work. The story of the battle of Mission Ridge is
struck with immortality already; let the leader of the
Fourth Corps bear it company.

That the center yet lies along its silent line is still
true; in five minutes it will be the wildest fiction. Let
us take that little breath of grace for just one glance at
the surroundings, since we shall have neither heart nor
eyes for it again. Did ever battle have so vast a cloud
of witnesses! The hive-shaped hills have swarmed.

Clustered like bees, blackening the house-tops, lining the fortifications, over yonder across the theatre, in the seats with the Catilines—everywhere, an hundred thousand beholders. Their souls are in their eyes. Not a murmur that you can hear. It is the most solemn congregation that ever stood up in the presence of the GOD of battles. I think of Bunker Hill as I stand here; of the thousands who witnessed that immortal struggle, and fancy there is a parallel. I think, too, that the chair of every man of them all will stand vacant against the wall to-morrow,—for to-morrow is Thanksgiving,—and around the fireside they must give thanks without him; if they can.

At half-past three a group of Generals, whose names will need no "Old Mortality" to chisel them anew, stood upon Orchard Knob. The hero of Vicksburg was there, calm, clear, persistent, far-seeing. Thomas, the sterling and sturdy; Meigs, Hunter, Granger, Reynolds. Clusters of humbler mortals were there too, but it was anything but a turbulent crowd; the voice naturally fell into a subdued tone, and even young faces took on the gravity of later years. An order was given, and in an instant the Knob was cleared like a ship's deck for action. At twenty minutes of four Granger stood upon the parapet by Bridges' Battery; the bugle swung idly at the bugler's

side, the warbling fife and grumbling drum unheard:—
there was to be *louder* talk—six guns at intervals of
two seconds the signal to advance. Strong and steady
his voice rang out: "Number one, fire! Number two,
fire! Number three, fire!"—it seemed to me the
tolling of the clock of destiny—and when at "Number
six, fire!" the roar throbbed out with the flash, you
should have seen the dead line that had been lying
behind the works all day, all night, all day again, come
to resurrection in the twinkling of an eye, leap like a
blade from its scabbard and sweep with a two-mile
stroke toward the Ridge. From divisions to brigades,
from brigades to regiments, the order ran. A minute,
and the skirmishers deploy; a minute, and the first
great drops begin to patter along the line; a minute,
and the musketry is in full play like the crackling
whips of a hemlock fire; men go down here and there,
before your eyes; the wind lifts the smoke and drifts
it away over the top of the Ridge; everything is too
distinct; it is fairly *palpable;* you can touch it with
your hand. The divisions of Wood and Sheridan are
wading breast-deep in the valley of death.

I never can tell you what it was like. They pushed
out, leaving nothing behind them. There was no
reservation in that battle. On moves the line of skirmishers, like a heavy frown, and after it, at quick time,

the splendid columns. At right of us and left of us and front of us, you can see the bayonets glitter in the sun. You cannot persuade yourself that Bragg was wrong, a day or two ago, when, seeing Hooker moving in, he said, "now we shall have a Potomac review;" that this is not the parade he prophesied; that it is of a truth the harvest of death to which they go down. And so through the fringe of woods went the line. Now, out into the open ground they burst into the double-quick. Shall I call it a Sabbath day's journey, or a long half mile? To me, that watched, it seemed endless as eternity, and yet they made it in thirty minutes. The tempest that now broke upon their heads was terrible. The enemy's fire burst out of the rifle-pits from base to summit of Mission Ridge; five batteries of Parrotts and Napoleons opened along the crest. Grape and canister and shot and shell sowed the ground with rugged iron and garnished it with the wounded and the dead. But steady and strong our columns moved on.

> "By heaven! It was a splendid sight to see,
>   For one who had no friend, no brother there,"

but to all loyal hearts, alas, and thank GOD, those men were friend and brother, both in one.

And over their heads, as they went, Forts Wood and Negley struck straight out like mighty pugilists right

and left, raining their iron blows upon the Ridge from
base to crest; Forts Palmer and King took up the
quarrel, and Moccasin Point cracked its fiery whips and
lashed the surly left till the wolf cowered in its corner
with a growl. Bridges' Battery, from Orchard Knob
below, thrust its ponderous fists in the face of the
enemy, and planted blows at will. Our artillery was
doing splendid service. It laid its shot and shell
wherever it pleased. Had giants carried them by hand
they could hardly have been more accurate. All along
the mountain's side, in the enemy's rifle-pits, on the
crest, they fairly dotted the Ridge. Granger leaped
down, sighted a gun, and in a moment, right in front,
a great volume of smoke, like "the cloud by day,"
lifted off the summit from among the batteries, and
hung motionless, kindling in the sun. The shot had
struck a caisson and that was its dying breath. In five
minutes away floated another. A shell went crashing
through a building in the cluster that marked Bragg's
headquarters; a second killed the skeleton horses of a
battery at his elbow; a third scattered a gray mass as
if it had been a wasp's nest.

And all the while our lines were moving on; they
had burned through the woods and swept over the
rough and rolling ground like a prairie fire. Never
halting, never faltering, they charged up to the first

rifle-pits with a cheer, forked out the foe with their bayonets, and lay there panting for breath. If the thunder of guns had been terrible, it was now growing sublime; it was like the footfall of GOD on the ledges of cloud. Our forts and batteries still thrust out their mighty arms across the valley; the guns that lined the arc of the crest full in our front, opened like the fan of Lucifer and converged their fire. It was rifles and musketry; it was grape and canister; it was shell and shrapnel. Mission Ridge was volcanic; a thousand torrents of red poured over its brink and rushed together to its base. And our men were there, halting for breath! And still the sublime diapason rolled on. Echoes that never waked before, roared out from height to height, and called from the far ranges of Waldron's Ridge to Lookout. As for Mission Ridge, it had jarred to such music before; it was the "sounding-board" of Chicamauga; it was behind us then; it frowns and flashes in our faces to-day. The old Army of the Cumberland was there; it breasted the storm till the storm was spent, and left the ground it held; the old Army of the Cumberland is here! It shall roll up the Ridge like a surge to its summit, and sweep triumphant down the other side. That memory and hope may have made the heart of many a blue-coat beat like a drum. "Beat," did I say? The feverish heart of the

battle beats on; fifty-eight guns a minute, by the
watch, is the rate of its terrible throbbing. That hill,
if you climb it, will appal you. Furrowed like a
summer-fallow,—bullets as if an oak had shed them;
trees clipped and shorn, leaf and limb, as with the
knife of some heroic gardener pruning back for richer
fruit. How you attain the summit, weary and breathless, I wait to hear; how *they* went up in the teeth of
the storm no man can tell!

And all this while prisoners have been streaming out
from the rear of our lines like the tails of a cloud of
kites. Captured and disarmed, they needed nobody to
set them going. The fire of their own comrades was
like spurs in a horse's flanks, and amid the tempest of
their own brewing, they ran for dear life, until they
dropped like quails into the Federal rifle-pits and were
safe. But our gallant legions are out in the storm; they
have carried the works at the base of the Ridge; they
have fallen like leaves in winter weather. Blow, dumb
bugles!

Sound the recall! "Take the rifle-pit," was the
order, and it is as empty of enemies as the tombs
of the prophets. Shall they turn their backs to the
blast? Shall they sit down under the eaves that drip
iron? Or shall they climb to the cloud of death above
them, and pluck out its lightnings as they would straws
from a sheaf of wheat? And now the arc of fire on

the crest grows fiercer and longer. The reconnoissance
of Monday had failed to develop the heavy metal of
the enemy. The dull fringe of the hill kindles with
the flash of great guns. I count the fleeces of white
smoke that dot the Ridge, as battery after battery
opens upon our line, until from the ends of the growing
arc they sweep down upon it in mighty X's of fire. I
count till that devil's girdle numbers thirteen batteries,
and my heart cries out: "Great GOD, when shall the
end be!" There is a poem I learned in childhood, and
so did you: it is Campbell's "Hohenlinden." One line
I never knew the meaning of until I read it written
along that hill! It has lighted up the whole poem for
me with the glow of battle forever:

> "And louder than the bolts of heaven,
>   Far flashed the red artillery!"

At this moment the commanding General's aids are
dashing out with an order; they radiate over the field
to left, right and front: "Take the Ridge if you can"
—and so it went along the line. But the advance had
already set forth without it. Stout-hearted Wood, the
iron-gray veteran, is rallying on his men; stormy
Turchin is delivering brave words in bad English;
Sheridan—little "Phil"—you may easily look down
upon him without climbing a tree, and see one of the
most gallant leaders of the age —is riding to and fro

along the first line of rifle-pits, as calmly as a chess-player. An aid rides up with the order. " Avery, that flask," said the General. Quietly filling the pewter cup, Sheridan looks up at the battery that frowns above him, by Bragg's headquarters, shakes his cap amid that storm of everything that kills, when you could hardly hold your hand without catching a bullet in it, and with a " how are you?" tosses off the cup. The blue battle-flag of the enemy fluttered a response to the cool salute, and the next instant the battery let fly its six guns showering Sheridan with earth. Allud-ing to that compliment with anything but a blank cartridge, the General said in his quiet way, " I thought it d—d ungenerous!" The recording angel will drop a tear upon the word for the part he played that day. Wheeling toward the men, he cheered them to the charge, and made at the hill like a bold-riding hunter; they were out of the rifle-pits and into the tempest and struggling up the steep, before you could get breath to tell it, and so they were throughout the inspired line.

And now you have before you one of the most startling episodes of the war; I cannot render it in words; dictionaries are beggarly things. But I may tell you they did not storm that mountain as you would think. They dash out a little way, and then slacken; they creep up, hand over hand, loading and firing, and wavering and halting, from the first line of works toward the second; they burst into a charge with a cheer and go over it. Sheets of flame baptize them; plunging shot tear away comrades on left and right; it is no longer shoulder to shoulder; it is GOD for us all? Under tree-trunks, among rocks, stumbling over the dead, struggling with the living; facing the steady fire of eight thousand infantry poured down upon their heads as if it were the old historic curse from heaven, they wrestle with the Ridge. Ten, fifteen, twenty minutes go by like a reluctant century. The batteries roll like a drum; between the second and the last line of works is the torrid zone of the battle; the hill sways up like a wall before them at an angle of forty-five degrees, but our brave mountaineers are clambering steadily on—up—upward still! You may think it strange, but I would not have recalled those men if I could. They would have lifted you, as they lifted me, in full view of the region of heroic grandeur; they seemed to be spurning the dull earth under their feet, and going up to do Homeric battle with the greater gods.

And what do these men follow? If you look you shall see that the thirteen thousand are not a rushing herd of human creatures; that along the Gothic roof of the Ridge a row of inverted V's is slowly moving up

almost in line, a mighty lettering on the hill's broad
side. At the angles of those V's is something that
glitters like a wing. Your heart gives a great bound
when you think what it is—*the regimental flag*—and
glancing along the front count fifteen of those colors
that were borne at Pea Ridge, waved at Shiloh, glorified at Stone River, riddled at Chicamauga. Nobler
than Cæsar s rent mantle are they all! And up move
the banners, now fluttering like a wounded bird, now
faltering, now sinking out of sight. Three times the
flag of the 27th Illinois goes down. And you know
why. Three dead color-sergeants lie just there, but the
flag is immortal—thank GOD!—and up it comes again,
and the V's move on. At the left of Wood, three regiments of Baird—Turchin, the Russian thunderbolt, is
there—hurl themselves against a bold point strong with
rebel works; for a long quarter of an hour three flags
are perched and motionless on a plateau under the
frown of the hill. Will they linger forever? I give a
look at the sun behind me; it is not more than a hand's
breadth from the edge of the mountain; its level rays
bridge the valley from Chattanooga to the Ridge with
beams of gold; it shines in the hostile faces; it brings
out the Federal blue; it touches up the flags. Oh, for
the voice that could bid that sun stand still! I turn
to the battle again; those three flags have taken flight.

They are upward bound! The men of the 88th Illinois were swept by an enfilading fire; Colonel Chandler seized the colors; they steadied into rock and swept the enemy before them with a broom of bayonets; it cost them fifty of the rank and file and two Lieutenants. Colonel Jacques, of the 73d, Barrett, of the 44th, Marsh, of the 74th, Dunlap, of the 51st—who the boys delight to say is "fashionable in a fight"—all wounded, and all Illinois.

The race of the flags is growing every moment more terrible. There at the right, in Colonel Sherman's brigade, a strange thing catches the eye; one of the inverted V's is turning right side up! The men struggling along the converging lines to overtake the flag have distanced it, and there the colors are, sinking down in the center between the rising flanks. The line wavers like a great billow, and up comes the banner again, as if it heaved on a surge's shoulder! The iron sledges beat on. Hearts, loyal and brave, are on the anvil all the way from base to summit of Mission Ridge, but those dreadful hammers never intermit. Swarms of bullets sweep the hill; you can count twenty-eight balls in one little tree. Things are growing desperate up aloft; the enemy tumble rocks upon the rising line; they light the fuses and roll shells down the steep; they load the guns with handfuls of cartridges in their haste; and as if there were powder in the word, they shout "Chicamauga!" down upon the mountaineers. But it would not all do, and just as the sun, weary of the scene, was sinking out of sight, with magnificent bursts all along the line, exactly as you have seen the crested seas leap up at the breakwater, the advance surged over the crest, and in a minute those flags fluttered along the fringe where fifty guns were kenneled. GOD bless the flag!

What colors were first upon the mountain battlement I dare not try to say; bright Honor's self may be proud to bear—bear?—nay, proud to *follow* the hindmost. Foot by foot they had fought up the steep slippery with much blood; let them go to glory together. But this I can declare: the 79th Indiana, of Wood's division, fairly ran over the rifle-pits, and left its whole line in the rear, and its breathless color-bearer led the way. But a few steps between him and the summit, he grasped a little tree that bravely clung there, and away he went, hand over hand, like a sailor up the shrouds, and shook his exultant flag above the crest. This I can declare: John Cheevers, of the 88th Illinois, planted his flag by Bragg's headquarters, and it kindled there in the setting sun, at the very heels of the enemy. A minute, and they were all there, fluttering along the Ridge from left to right. The routed hordes rolled off to the north, rolled off to the east, like the clouds of a worn-out storm. Bragg, ten minutes before, was putting men back into the rifle-pits. His gallant gray was straining a nerve for him now, and the man rode on horseback into "Dixie's" bosom, who, arrayed in some prophet's discarded mantle, foretold, on Monday, that the Yankees' would leave Chattanooga in five days. They left it in three, and by the way of Mission Ridge, straight over the mountains as their forefathers went! As Sheridan rode up to the guns, the heels of Breckenridge's horse glittered in the last rays of sunshine. That crest was hardly "well off with the old love before it was on with the new."

But the scene on that narrow plateau can never be painted. As the blue-coats surged over its edge, cheer on cheer rang like bells through the valley of the Chicamauga. Men flung themselves exhausted upon the ground. They laughed and wept, shook hands, embraced; turned round and did all four over again. It was as wild as a carnival. The General was received with a shout. "Soldiers," he said, "you ought to be court-martialed, every man of you. I ordered you to take the rifle-pits and you scaled the mountain!" but it was not Mars' horrid front exactly with which he said it, for his cheeks were wet with tears as honest as the blood that reddened all the route. Wood uttered

words that rang like " Napoleons," and Sheridan, the
rowels at his horse's flanks, was ready for a dash down
the Ridge with a " view halloo " for a fox hunt.

But you must not think this was all there was of the
scene on the crest, for fight and frolic were strangely
mingled. Not a gray-coat had dreamed a man of us
all would live to reach the summit, and when a little
wave of the Federal cheer rolled up and broke over the
crest, they defiantly cried : " hurrah and be d—d ;" the
next minute the 65th Ohio followed the voice, the
enemy delivered their fire, and tumbled down in the
rifle-pits. No sooner had the soldiers scrambled to the
Ridge and straightened themselves, than up muskets
and away they blazed. One of them, fairly beside
himself between laughing and crying, seemed puzzled
at which end of his piece he should load, and so, aban-
doning the gun and the problem together, he made a
catapult of himself and fell to hurling stones after the
enemy. And he said, as he threw—well, " our army,"
you know, " swore terribly in Flanders." Bayonets
glinted and muskets rattled. Sheridan's horse was
killed under him ; " Richard " was not in his *role*, and
so he leaped upon a rebel gun for want of another.
The artillerists are driven from their batteries at the
edge of the sword and the point of the bayonet ; two
guns are swung around upon their old masters. But

there is nobody to load them. Light and heavy artillery do not belong to the wingèd kingdom. Two
infantry men claiming to be old artillerists, volunteer.
Granger turns captain of the guns, and—right about
wheel!—in a moment they are growling after the flying
enemy. I say flying, but that is figurative. The many
run like Spanish merinoes, but the few fight like lions
at bay; they load and fire as they retreat; they are
fairly scorched out of position. It was so where
Turchin struck them, and so where Wood and Sheridan
gave them the iron glove. Colonel Harker is slashing
away with his sabre in a ring of foes. Down goes his
horse under him; they have him on the hip; one of
them is taking deliberate aim, when up rushes Lieutenant Johnson, of the 42d Illinois, claps a pistol to one
ear and roars in at the other, "Who the h—l are you
shooting at?" The fellow drops his piece, gasps out,
"I surrender," and the next instant the gallant Lieutenant falls sharply wounded. He is a "roll of honor"
officer straight up from the ranks. A little German in
Wood's division is pierced like the lid of a pepper-box,
but is neither dead nor wounded. "See here," he says,
rushing up to a comrade, "a pullet hit te preech of
mine gun—a pullet in mine bocket pook—a pullet in
mine goat-tail—dey shoots me three, five dime, and by
tam I gives dem h—l yet!"

But I can render you no idea of the battle caldron that boiled on the plateau. An incident, here and there, I have given you, and you must fill out the picture for yourself. Dead soldiers lay thick around Bragg's headquarters and along the ridge. Scabbards, broken arms, artillery horses, wrecks of gun carriages, bloody garments, strewed the scene; and, tread lightly, oh, true-hearted, the boys in blue are lying there; no more the sounding charge; no more the brave wild cheer; and never for them, sweet as the breath of new-mown hay in the old home fields, "the Soldier's Return from the War." A little waif of a drummer boy, somehow drifted up the mountain in the surge, lies there, his pale face upward, a blue spot on his breast. Muffle his drum for the poor child and his mother.

Our troops met one cordial welcome on the height. How the old Tennessecan that gave it managed to get there nobody knows, but there he was, grasping Colonel Harker's hand, and saying, while the tears ran down his face, "GOD be thanked! I *knew* the Yankees would fight!" With the receding flight and swift pursuit the battle died away in murmurs, far down the valley of the Chicamauga; Sheridan was again in the saddle, and with his command spurring on after the enemy. Tall columns of smoke were rising at the left. The enemy were burning a train of stores a mile long.

In the exploding caissons we had "the cloud by day," and now we were having "the pillar of fire by night." The sun, the golden dish of the scales that balance day and night, had hardly gone down when up, beyond Mission Ridge, rose the silver side, for that night it was full moon. The troubled day was done. A Federal officer sat in the seat of the man who, on the very Saturday before the battle, had sent a flag to the lines with these words:

"Humanity would dictate the removal of all non-combatants from Chattanooga, as I am about to shell the city!"

—Sat there and announced to the Fourth Corps the congratulations and thanks just placed in his hands, from the commander of the Department.

"BRAGG'S HEADQUARTERS, MISSION RIDGE,
November 25, 1863.

"In conveying to you this distinguished recognition of your signal gallantry in carrying, through a terrible storm of iron, a mountain crowned with batteries and encircled with rifle-pits, I am constrained to express my own admiration of your noble conduct, and am proud to tell you that the veteran Generals from other fields who witnessed your heroic bearing, place your assault and triumph among the most brilliant achievements of the war. Thanks, Soldiers! You have made, this day, a glorious page of history.

"GORDON GRANGER."

There was a species of poetic justice in it all that would have made the prince of dramatists content. The ardor of the men had been quenchless; there had been three days of fitful fever, and after it, alas, a multitude slept well. The work on the right, left and center cost us full four thousand killed and wounded. There is a tremble of the lip but a flash of pride in the eye as the soldier tells with how many he went in—how expressive is that "went in!" Of a truth it was wading in deep waters—with how few he came out. I cannot try to swing the burden clear from any heart by throwing into the scale upon the other side the dead-weight of fifty-two pieces of captured artillery, ten thousand stand of arms and heaps of dead enemies, or by driving upon it a herd of seven thousand prisoners. Nothing of all this can lighten that burden a single ounce, but those three days' work brought Tennessee to resurrection; set the flag, that fairest blossom in all this flowery world, to blooming in its native soil again.

That splendid march from the Federal line of battle to the crest, was made in one hour and five minutes, but it was a grander march toward the end of carnage; a glorious campaign of sixty-five minutes toward the white borders of peace. It made that fleeting November afternoon imperishable. Let the struggle be known as the Battle of Mission Ridge, and now that calmer days have come, men make pilgrimage and women smile again among the mountains of the Cumberland, but they need no guide. Rust may have eaten the guns; the graves of the heroes may have subsided like waves weary of their troubling; the soldier and his leader may have lain down together, but there, embossed upon the globe, Mission Ridge will stand its fitting monument forever.

THANKSGIVING AT CHATTANOOGA.

The day after the battle was Thanksgiving, and we had services in Chattanooga—sad, solemn, grand. The church-bells hung dumb in their towers, indeed, and you shall know why in its time, but for all that, there were chimes so grand that men uncovered their heads as they heard them. At twelve o'clock the great guns at Fort Wood began to toll. Civilians said, " Can they be at it again?"—and soldiers said, " The guns are not shotted, and the sound is too regular for work." I hastened out to the Fort, and the guns chimed on. A dim impression I had received before brightened as I stood upon the parapet and looked over the scene. What it was like flashed upon me in a moment: the valley was a grand cathedral, Fort Wood the pulpit of the mighty minster, and far down the descending aisle in front rose Orchard Knob the altar. The dead were lying there, far out to the eastern wall, and GOD's chandelier hung high in the dome. They were the accents of praise I was hearing; thirty-four syllables of thanksgiving the guns were saying: "Oh, give thanks unto the LORD, for He is good; for His mercy endureth forever!" And the hills took up the anthem and struck sublimely in; from the Ridge it came back, "give thanks unto the LORD," and Waldron's height uttered it, "for His mercy endureth," and Lookout Valley sang aloud, "forever, forever," and all the mountains cried, "Amen!"

And the churches of Chattanooga had congregations. Those who composed them had come silent and suffering and of steady heart; had come upon stretchers; come in men's arms, like infants to the christening; ambulances had been drawing up to the church-doors all night with their burdens, and within those walls it looked one great altar of sacrifice. The nearest of these edifices is hardly a dozen paces from my quarters, and I go out and sit upon its step in the sun. It is the same building wherein the gifted Murdoch, only a few days before, had given his splendid renderings of drama and lyric. I do not hear the music of his voice, neither do I hear a moan. The doors are

noiselessly opening and closing, and I see pale faces
—bloody garments. Right hands lie in the porch that
have offended and been cut off; castaway feet are
there, too, but there is nothing about sinning feet in
the Sermon on the Mount! It is not the house of
wailing on whose threshold I am waiting; it is the
house of patience. Five still figures, covered by five
brown blankets, are ranged on the floor beside me.
Their feet are manacled with bits of slender twine, but
a spider's thread could hold them. I lift a corner of
the blankets and look at the quiet faces. By the gray
coat I see that one is a dead rebel. Do men look
nearer alike when dead than when alive? Else how
could it have chanced that one of these sleepers in
Federal blue should resemble him nearly enough for
both to have been "twinned at a birth?" They are
not wounded in the face, and so there is nothing to
shock you; they fell in their full strength. Tread
lightly, lest they be not dead, but sleeping. The
silence within oppresses me; it seems as if an accent
of pain from some sufferer in that solemn church would
be a welcome sound, and I think of a brave bird
wounded unto death, that I have held in my hand, its
keen eye undimmed and full upon me, throbbing with
the pain and the dying, and yet so silent!

But I am not trying to write a poem, and so, at the
risk of startling you, I must tell you that the grating
sounds of busy life around are set to no minor key, in
keeping with the scenes.   Nature never sympathizes
with human suffering, though in our vanity we sometimes think she does, and I am inclined to believe that
man and nature are often much alike.   Three or four
little Africans—by some accident born unbleached—are
playing " hop-scotch " on the sunny slope at the corner
of the church, gurgling like japanned water-spouts with
laughter, and exploding now and then into an unmiti-
gated " yah, yah."   A couple of soldiers are going by,
while several white-wood coffins are being borne up to
the porch.   They stop, give a glance, and one says to
the other, " I say, Jack, our boys killed on Mission
Ridge, yesterday, are thundering lucky,—don't you
think so? "   " Why? " said his comrade.   " Because
they can all have wooden overcoats! "   It was no
heartless jest, as you might fancy, but an old campaigner's way of putting things.   Alas, for the battle-
fields to whose heroes the luxury of a coffin must be
denied, and yet they sleep as sweetly close folded in
the earth.   I go around the church; a soldier has his
foot upon a spade, digging a hole.   I ask him its
purpose.   He never looks up, but keeps crowding the
rusty blade craunchingly into the red earth, and tosses

the answer to me sullenly over his left shoulder: "buryin' legs!" I look down and see uncertain shapes beneath a blanket lying on the ground, go to the right-about, and walk gently away. The ragged cut he gave me was even more painful than the Timbuctooan explosives, but when I think of it, it is only the blunt edge of use with which he did it. He would have played sexton to his own limbs as coolly.

You wander down into Main street; hospitals there. You go up the hill by the Market House; hospitals *there*. You see thirty unarmed men drawn up on the sidewalk, a Lieutenant commanding. Four soldiers are bringing weapons strange to them across the street; their arms are full of shovels: you see the builders of the doomsday houses; it is the Shovel Brigade. An order is given, and away they move, up the hill, out of town, to the eastward. They are not sad men, as the lamenting Rachels would believe, but cheerful, if not smiling. Shall we follow them to the place of graves? There it is, the slope turned towards the setting sun, that even now is "promising a glorious morrow;" a strange piece of check-work; a spot already honey-combed with graves. And the Shovel Brigade begins to widen the breadth of the solemn tillage; doing for dead comrades what, for anything they know or think, somebody may do for them the next day or the next.

There were seven hundred and forty-two graves in that one place, on Thanksgiving night.

Going slowly homeward we meet them coming. And what *is* them? The plaintive cry of fifes—it is almost a woman's wail—and the moan of muffled drums come up from the laps of the little valleys of Chattanooga. It is the lament of Ramah here in Tennessee! I have heard the splendid bands in great cities, and the sighing of organs over the dead, but that music among the mountains I cannot describe. There are tears in the tones, and will be till my dying day. An ambulance bearing the dead, and then a dozen comrades following after, two by two, another ambulance and more comrades; but no flags, no pomp, only those fifes, like the voice of girls that sing "China." The ambulances are lightened. Dirge and "Dead March" are dropped into the graves, and back they go to a quickstep, here, there, everywhere; the fifes warble like birds in spring; life and cheer tread close on death and gloom. And so it went, Thursday and Friday and Saturday. And such was Thanksgiving at Chattanooga.

AFTER THE BATTLE.

When a furnace is in blast, the red fountain sparkles and plays like a mountain spring, and the rude surroundings brighten to the peak of the rough rafters with a strange beauty. When the fire is out, and the black and rugged masses of dull iron lie dead upon the ground, with a dumb and stubborn resistance, who would dream that they had ever leaped with life and light?

A battle and a furnace are alike. It is wonderful how dull natures brighten and grow costly in the glow of battle; how the sterling worth and wealth there are in them shine out, and the common man stands transfigured, his heart in his hand and his foot in the realm of grandeur. But ah, when the fire is out, and the scarred earth is heaped with rigid clay, the black mouths of the guns speechless, mighty hammers and no hands, the wild hurrah died away, and all the splendid action of the charge vanished from the field, and you wander among the dull remainders, the dead embers of the intensest life and glow that swept your soul out, only yesterday, and drifted it on with the skirmish line, you begin to know what those words mean—"after the battle."

I feel like taking up the story just where I left it, on Wednesday night at sunset, when our flags flapped like eagles' wings, and the wild cry of triumph quivered along the mountain. Standing on the edge of the field in the moonlight, calm as a field of wheat, stretches the rough valley that jarred with the rush and whirl of the battle. From away beyond the ridge, three miles out to Chicamauga station, the dropping shots from Sheridan's guns faintly punctuate the silence, but here, listen as you will, you can hear no sound but the click of ambulance wheels, slowly rolling in with their mangled burdens: no sigh, no groan, nothing but the sobbing lapse of the Tennessee.

It is strange that a battle almost always lies between two breadths of sleep: the dreamless slumber into which men fall upon its eve: the calm repose they sink in at its end. Night fairly held its breath above the camps; the wing of silence was over them all. Then came Thursday morning, bright and beautiful. You go out to the field; and you keep saying over and over, "after the battle—after the battle." Men prone upon their faces in death's deep abasement; here one, his head pillowed upon his folded arms; there one, his cheek pressed upon a stone, as was Jacob's at Bethel; yonder one, his fingers stiffened round his musket. Now you pass where a "butternut" and a true blue have gone down together, the arm of the one flung over the other; where a young boy of fifteen lies face upward, both hands clasped over his heart. The sun has touched the frost that whitened his hair, as if he had grown old in a night, and it hangs like tears fresh-fallen upon his cheeks; where a Lieutenant grasps a bush, as if he died vainly feeling for a little hold upon earth and life, where a stained trail leads you to a shelter behind a rock, and a dead Captain who had crept way out of sight and fallen asleep; where friends and foes lie in short windrows, as if Death had begun the harvest and had wearied of the work. And so, through the valley and up the Ridge, in every attitude lie the unburied dead; lie just as they fell in the battle. And those faces are not what you would think: hardly one distorted with any passion; almost as white and calm as Ben Adhem's dream of peace; many brightened with something like a smile; a few strangely beautiful. Wounded ones that escaped the moonlight search have lain silently waiting for morning, without murmur or complaint; glad they are alive; not grieved they are wounded, for "did we not take the Ridge?" they say. Thus did the old soldierly spirit of one flash up like an expiring candle, and go out right there on the field as he spoke; he died with the last word on his lips, and "went up higher."

Spots all along that terrible mountain route are waiting some poet's breath to blossom with flowers immortal.   Here, by this gray rock, lay the soldier, one
shoulder shattered like a piece of potter's clay, and
thus urged two comrades who had halted to bear him
to the rear: " Don't stop for me—I'm of no account—
for GOD'S sake, push right up with the boys! "—and on
they went and left him weltering in his bloody vest-
ments.   Between the first and second ranges of the
enemy's works, right in the flush of the charge, a Captain fell, and two men came to his aid.   " Don't wait
here," he said; " go back to your company; one useless
man is enough; don't make it three."   Just then a
cheer floated down the mountain as they took the
rifle-pit.   " Don't you hear that?" he cried; "march!"
and away they went.   Such incidents as these strow all
the way from base to crest; happening in an instant,
lost and forgotten in the whirlwind; worthy, every one
of them, of a medal in gold; worthy, every one of
them, of a place in history and hearts.

A MOUNTAIN CAMP.

What mighty names of paltry things war thrusts into
history, and leaves them there like flies preserved in
amber.   There is Stevenson.   What columns have been

written about it—nay, what columns have converged to
it, and yet Stevenson is a straggling, ragged little town,
of a couple of dozen buildings, that used to hang about
the intersection of the Memphis and Charleston, and
Nashville and Chattanooga Railroads, to see the cars go
by. It was dropped down fairly within the borders of
Alabama, among the rocky ledges, some six miles from
the Tennessee River, and there is nothing contemptible
about Stevenson but Stevenson's self. The Cumberland hills, laid up in rock and sprinkled thickly with
cedars, are piled very grandly about it, all rough with
monuments of Nature's make, the gray stones set up
on end, strangely carved by the action of some perished
flood, and reminding you of the lonely graveyards of
the Covenanters, the inscriptions all washed away.
Tumbling into the eddy of mules and elbows in the
dark, I found quarters with a fighting regiment, the 3d
Ohio. Here, turning a new leaf, there lay a new experience. Ten thousand men are encamped around us.
Far up the hills, reddening the cedars, twinkle the
camp-fires; flocks of tents dot the slopes; clusters of
mules and horses, tied to trees, present peripheries of
heels everywhere; valley and hill are tangled in a net-
work of paths; fat bacon is complaining from the ends
of ramrods; the aroma of coffee struggles with baser
odors; perched upon the ledges, at length beneath the

trees, under canvas and in open air—everywhere soldiers.   Here a boy has just planked the ace and taken
the "trick;" or finished the letter to the girl he left
behind him, or lighted his pipe, or wrung out his shirt,
or shaken up his cedar boughs for a shake-down; he is
playing the flute; he is drawing the long bow; he is
talking over Perryville or Murfreesboro.   Here, by an
inch of candle, a cluster of two heads hangs over a
book.   There, around a half-cord of bread and a pile
of·russet slabs of bacon, and sacks of sugar and rice, a
group is gathered, little, smoky kettle, tin cup, haversack, in hand.   Somebody, eager to see, skips up on
somebody's slab of bacon with his bare feet, and the
distribution is effected.   Up through the night wails the
bugle; along the valley rolls the beat of drums; down
from the crags float, "When this cruel war is over,"
"Oh, take your time, Miss Lucy," and the loud laugh
and the tough word.   The money changers follow the
army; trade bustles up on the heels of war; a dumb-
watch swings from the flap of a tent door; a clothing
store is anchored by a tent-pin; nick-nacks and noth-
ings go at starvation prices; water suspected of lemon,
a dime a thimble-full; pencils whose lead, unlike Federal
bullets, does not go quite through, are good for a quarter; and, as the apothecary says, "and so on."

    If, like a cat, you step gingerly in the damp grass; if
you are given to touching things with the tips of your

fingers; if you are a disbeliever in the "peck of dirt" doctrine, and are rose-waterish and patent-leathered; if you rebel at tin plates, bayonet candle-sticks, bacon and hard-tack; in a word, if you have any "nonsense" about you, keep out of the camps; you are not fit for the army; you have not begun to find out what the Union is worth. A capital place is the army to get rid of notions; to settle loose joints into solid independence; to fall in love with mother earth and free air.

A SOLDIER'S MORNING.

Morning breaks strangely and musically in camp. Not a familiar sound in it all; no bells, no lowing herds, no "cock's shrill clarion," no rattling pavements, no opening doors. Turn out before the camps are astir, and just as the whole family of canvas, Sibley cone, "wall," and that bit of a kennel, the "dog" tent, begin to show gray in the dawn. The colors at headquarters droop heavy and damp. All around you, as far as the eye can reach, it seems a badly harvested field that has grown a monstrous crop of men, now lying heads and points everywhere. By the calendar it is Sunday, but of pattern too narrow to lap over into Alabama in this year of grace and gunpowder, '63.

And now the music begins: floating lightly over the top of the woods and the top of the morning, comes a strange Babel of melody; the cat-bird whines through the song of sparrow and robin, and the bell of the bobolink rings out over the scream of the jay. And the little brown master of this brisk skirmish of discord and melody sits on the uttermost green billow of summer—the little epicure with a passion for beefsteak and fat spiders. I had forgotten until the minute that I was in the home of the mocking-bird, that winged polyglot of the South. These birds sing out the night and the moonlight, and have a monotonous note for that hour. They seem to be posted like sentries, and soldiers as they ride hear them passing the little signals along from grove and thicket to grove and thicket again, and are thus challenged by each unseen picket, until the daybreak and the song-break come grandly in together.

By and by, from field, wood and hill, come the sweet notes of the *reveille;* bugle echoes bugle, the fifes warble up through the roaring surf of the drums, and the dear, old swell of a full band rolls over the tops of the trees from an unseen camp. In singular contrast to all this, an anomalous gamut of groans, neighs strangled in the making, and half-human snorts, runs round the whole landscape. It is the hideous morning welcome of the immense cordon of mules to the rustle of the morning forage. Flags flutter out, and blue threads of smoke curl up along the camps; the clink of the but-ends of bayonets, beating the little bag full of Rio, give you the merry music of the soldier's coffee-mill; little tin pails and camp-kettles go tinkling about. You are bugled to breakfast, bugled to guard-mounting, bugled to dinner, bugled to battle, bugled to bed, the bass-drums the while giving three vicious growls at your heels as you go. These "calls" are pleasant little devices for translating curt English orders into music. Brigades move to them, and cavalry charge; they sound clear and shrill on the field of battle, and the horse and his rider obey them together.

But there is one "call" sounded just after breakfast, before the tent of the surgeon, that summons up, in camp phrase, the "cripples" for treatment. It is not an ugly strain, and may be rendered into words that exhaust at once the tune and its burden: "Come to qui-nine, come to qui-nine. Walk up quick, walk up quick—come to *qui-n-i-n-e !*"

EVERY DAY LIFE UNDER CANVAS.

If there are men in the world gifted with the most thorough self-reliance, American soldiers are the men. To fight in the grand anger of battle seems to me to require less manly fortitude than to bear without murmuring the swarm of little troubles that vex camp and march. No matter where or when you halt them they are at once at home. They know precisely what to do first, and they do it. I have seen them march into a strange region at dark, and almost as soon as fires would show well, they were twinkling all over the field, the Sibley cones rising like the work of enchantment everywhere, and the little dog-tents lying snug to the ground, as if, like the mushrooms, they had grown there, and the aroma of coffee and tortured bacon, suggesting creature comforts, and the whole economy of life in canvas cities moving as steadily on as if it had never intermitted. The movements of regiments are as blind as fate. Nobody can tell to-night where he will be to-morrow, and yet with the first glimmer of morning the camp is astir, and the preparations begin for staying there forever. An ax, a knife and a will are tools enough for a

soldier house-builder. He will make the mansion and
all its belongings of red cedar, from the ridge-pole to
the forestick, though a couple of dog-tents stretched
from wall to wall will make a roof worth thanking the
LORD for. Having been mason and joiner, he turns
cabinet-maker; there are his table, his chairs, his side-
board; he glides into upholstery, and there is his bed
of bamboo, as full of springs and comfort as a patent
mattress. He whips out a needle and turns tailor; he
is not above the mysteries of the sauce-pan and camp-
kettle; he can cook, if not quite like a Soyer, yet
exactly like a soldier, and you may believe that he can
eat you hungry when he is in trim for it. Cosy little
cabins, neatly fitted, are going up; here a boy is making
a fire-place, and quite artistically plastering it with the
inevitable red earth; he has found a crane somewhere
and swung up thereon a two-legged dinner-pot; there
a fellow is finishing out a chimney with brick from an
old kiln of secession proclivities; yonder a bower-house,
closely interwoven with evergreen, is almost ready for
the occupants, the avenues between the lines of tents
are cleared and smoothed—"policed," in camp phrase;
little seats with cedar awnings in front of the tents give
a cottage-look, while the interior, in a rude way, has a
genuine home-like air. The bit of a looking-glass hangs
against the cotton wall; a handkerchief of a carpet just

before the bunk marks the stepping-off place to the
land of dreams; a violin case is strung to a convenient
hook, flanked by a gorgeous picture of some hero of
somewhere, mounted upon a horse rampant and saltant,
"and what a length of tail behind!"

The business of living has fairly begun again. There
is hardly an idle moment, and save here and there a
man brushing up his musket, getting that "damned
spot" off his bayonet, burnishing his revolver, you
would not suspect that these men had but one terrible
errand. They are tailors, they are tinkers, they are
writers; fencing, boxing, cooking, eating, drilling,—
those who say that camp-life is a lazy life know little
about it. And then the reconnoissances "on private
account;" every wood, ravine, hill, field, is explored;
the productions, animal and vegetable, are inventoried,
and one day renders them as thoroughly conversant
with the region round about as if they had been dwell-
ing there a lifetime. Soldiers have interrogation points
in both eyes. They have tasted water from every
spring and well, estimated the corn to the acre, tried
the water-melons, bagged the peaches, knocked down
the persimmons, milked the cows, roasted the pigs,
picked the chickens; they know who lives here and
there and yonder, the whereabouts of the native boys,
the names of the native girls. If there is a curious cave,

a queer tree, a strange rock, anywhere about, they know it. You can see them with chisel, hammer and haversack, tugging up the mountain, or scrambling down the ravine, in a geological passion that would have won the right hand of fellowship from Hugh Miller, and home they come with specimens that would enrich a cabinet. The most exquisite fossil buds just ready to open, beautiful shells, rare minerals, are collected by these rough and dashing naturalists. If you think the rank and file have no taste and no love for the beautiful, it is time you remembered of what material they are made. Nothing will catch a soldier's eye quicker than a patch of velvet moss, or a fresh little flower, and many a letter leaves the camps enriched with faded souvenirs of these expeditions. I said that nothing will catch an old campaigner's eye quicker than a flower, but I was wrong,—a dirty, ragged *baby* will. I have seen a thirteen-dollar man expend a dollar for trinkets to hang about the neck of an urchin that at home and three years ago he would hardly have touched with the tongs. Do you say, it is for the mother's sake? You have only to see the bedraggled, coarse, lank, tobacco-chewing dam to abandon that idea, like a foundling, to the tender mercies of the first door-step.

But to come back to camp: talk of perfumed clouds of incense, there is nothing sweeter than a clear, bright red cedar fire; the mountain air is fairly laden with the fragrance Everything is red cedar, and a prairie man, as he sees the great camp-fires fed with hewn timbers of the precious wood, would about as soon think of cutting up his grand piano—seven octave or so—into fuel for the kitchen stove. The breath of the red cedar fires will float back to me like a pleasant memory, if ever I inhale again the sulphurous Tartarean gusts from the smothering beds of Illinois coal. Writing of fuel, you should see the fences melt away anywhere within a mile of camp; up goes the red cedar again, like the prophet, in a chariot of fire, and not enough left for a bow and arrow.

The work of improvement goes briskly on; a week has passed, and the boys seem settled for life. Just before tattoo, some night, down comes an order to march at five in the morning. A fine, drizzling rain has set in; a thick blanket of fog has been snugly tucked around the camp; the fires look large and red and cheerful; the boys are just ready to turn in when down comes the order. Nothing is as you would think; no complaints, no murmurings. no watching the night out. They are not to be cheated out of their sleep—not they; it takes your green recruits for that; every bundle of a blanket has a sleeping soldier in it; every knapsack has a drowsy head on it. At three the roll

of a drum straggles through the gloom; the camp is
awake; tents are struck, knapsacks packed, baggage
wagons loaded, mules untangled. Soldiers have
notions, and among them is the destruction of
their "improvements;" the bower-house crackles like
a volley of musketry, the cedar cottages are in flames,
the stools and tables are glowing coals, and if they
don't fiddle, as Nero did, while their Rome is burning—and as much of a Rome, too, as that was in the
time of the lupine brothers—at least they *eat*. A
soldier can starve patiently, but when he has a chance
he eats potently. Huddled around their little fires,
in the thick and turbid morning, the smutty kettles
bubble with the Arabic decoction as black as the
tents of the Sheik who threw dust on the beard of
his father: unhappy pork sizzles from ramrods, and
the boys take breakfast.

Some wise man proposed in Congress the substitu-
tion of tea for coffee in the army, and told the people
that the soldiers would welcome the change! A
tolerably fair specimen of theoretical, stay-at-home
wisdom, but not worth a Sabbath-day's journey of the
Queen of Sheba to look at. Coffee is their true *aqua
vitæ;* their solace and mainstay. When a boy cannot
drink his coffee, you may be sure he has done drinking
altogether. On a march, no sooner is a halt ordered,

than little fires begin to twinkle along the line; they
make coffee in five minutes, drink it in three, take a
drill at a hard cracker, and are refreshed.   Our comrades from " der Rhein" will squat phlegmatically
anywhere, even in line of battle.   No sooner has the
storm swept to some other part of the field, than the
kettles begin to boil, and amid stray bullets and
shattering shell, they take great swallows of heart and
coffee together.   It is Rhine wine, the soul of Gam-
brinus, " Switzer" and " Limberg" in one.

But it is five o'clock and a dingy morning; the
regiments march away in good cheer, the army-wagons
go streaming and swearing after them; the beat of the
drum grows fainter, the last straggler is out of sight;
the canvas city has vanished like a vision.   On such a
morning and amid such a scene I have loitered till it
seemed as if a busy city had been passing out of sight,
leaving nothing behind for all that life and light but
empty desolation.   Will you wonder much if I tell you
that I have watched such a vanishing with a pang of
regret; that the trampled field looked dim to me, worn
smooth and beautiful by the touch of those brave feet
whose owners have trod upon thorns with song—feet,
alas, how many, that shall never again in all this
coming and going world make music upon the old
thresholds?   And how many such sites of perished

cities this war has made; how many bonds of good fellowship have been rent to be united no more!

At home anywhere, I wrote, and I might well have added, and used to anything, the boys are. You would wonder, I think, to see men lie right down in the dusty road, under the full noon sun of Tennessee and Alabama, and fall asleep in a minute. I have passed hundreds of such sleepers. A dry spot is as good as a mattress; the flap of a blanket quite a downy pillow. You would wonder to see a whole army corps without a shred of a tent to bless themselves with, lying anywhere and everywhere in an all-night rain, and not a growl nor a grumble. I was curious to see whether the pluck and good nature were washed out of them, and so I made my way out of the snug, dry quarters I am ashamed to say I occupied, at five in the morning, to see what water had done for them. Nothing! Each soaked blanket hatched out as jolly a fellow as you would wish to see—muddy, dripping, half-foundered, forth they came, wringing themselves out as they went, with the look of a troop of wet-down roosters in a fall rain, plumage at half-mast, but hearts trumps every time. If they swore—and some did—it was with a half-laugh; the sleepy fires were stirred up; then came the inevitable coffee, and they were as good as new. "Blood is thicker than

water." I could never tire of telling you how like iron
—wrought iron—men can get to be, and half the
sympathy I had corked and labeled for the hardships
of soldiers evaporated when I came to see how like
rugged oaks they toughened into knots under them.
There is another light to the picture. The regiment
twelve hundred strong now stacks five hundred muskets. Bullets did not do it, but just the terrible sifting
process; the regiment is screened like grain; the
sturdiest manhood alone remains. Writing of downy
pillows, I noticed on that rainy morning, that one of
the boys did not hug mother earth quite as closely as
the rest; his head was well up, and when he shook
himself and whisked off the blanket he had lain upon,
I saw his pillow, and no duck ever dressed such
plumage; it was a little triangular piece of iron, the
fragment of some bit of machinery, through which
were thrust three iron rods some six inches in length.
It was first this queer tripod of a pillow, then a corner
of a blanket, then a pouring rain, and then a good,
hearty, all-night sleep. Never mind that feather the
wrong way in *your* pillow; thank GOD for the one
feather, pleasant dreams and good-night!

THE HOSPITAL AFTER THE BATTLE.

The Ohio at Louisville behind you, southward across Kentucky and Tennessee you look upon the region in the rear of the Army of the Cumberland, a breadth of three hundred and eight miles to the spurs of the mountains. That area once so lovely is dappled with those shadows strange and sad—the Hospitals of the Federal Army. At Chattanooga, at Bridgeport, at Stevenson, at Cowan, at Decherd, at Murfreesboro, at Nashville, strown all along the way are flocks of tents sacred to mercy and the soldier's sake. I wish I could bring you near enough to see them; that I could lift aside a fold in ward A here, or ward B there; that you might see the pale rows, each man upon his little couch, the white sheet setting close to the poor, thin limbs like the drapery of the grave. It would wonderfully magnify, I think, the work of the women of the North.

I would not take you to the Surgeon's quarters when the battle is beginning; when he lays off the green sash and the tinseled coat, and rolls up his sleeves, and spreads wide his cases filled with the terrible glitter of silver steel, and makes ready to work. They begin to

come in, slowly at first, one man nursing a shattered
arm, another borne by his comrades, three in an
ambulance, one on a stretcher; then faster and faster,
lying here, lying there, waiting each his terrible turn.
The silver steel grows cloudy and lurid; true right
arms are lopped like slips of golden willow; feet that
never turned from the foe, forever more without an
owner, strow the ground. The knives are busy, the
saws play; it is bloody work. Ah, the surgeon with
heart and head, with hand and eye fit for such a place,
is a prince among men; cool and calm, quick and
tender, he feels among the arteries and fingers the
tendons as if they were harp-strings. But the cloud
thunders and the spiteful rain patters louder and
fiercer, and the poor fellows come creeping away in
broken ranks like corn beaten down with the flails
of the storm. "My GOD!" cried a surgeon, as, looking up an instant from his work, he saw the mutilated
crowds borne in; "my GOD. are *all* my boys cut
down!" And yet it thundered and rained. A poor
fellow writhes and a smothered moan escapes him.
"Be patient, Jack," says the surgeon, cheerfully; "I'll
make you all right in a minute.' And what a meaning
there was in that "all right!" It was a right arm to
come off at the elbow, and "Jack" slipped off a ring
that clasped one of the poor, useless fingers that were

to blend with the earth of Alabama, and put it in his pocket! He was making ready for the "all right." *Does* Alabama mean "here we rest?" If so, how sad yet glorious have our boys made it, who sink to rest

"With all their country's wishes blest!"

Another sits up while the surgeon follows the bullet that had buried itself in his side; it is the work of an instant; no solemn council here, no lingering pause; the surgeon is bathed in patriot blood to his elbows, and the work goes on. An eye lies out upon a ghastly cheek, and silently the sufferer bides his time. "Well, Charley," says the doctor—he is dressing a wound as he talks—"What's the matter?" "Oh, not much, Doctor, only a hand off." Not unlike was the answer made to me by a poor fellow, at Bridgeport, shattered as a tree is by lightning; "how are you now?" I said. "*Bully!*" was the reply. You should have heard that word, as he gave it; vulgar as it used to seem, it grew manly and noble, and I shall never hear it again without a thought for the boy that uttered it, on the dusty slope of the Tennessee; the boy that sleeps the soldier's sleep within an hundred rods of the spot where I found him. And so it is everywhere; not a whimper nor a plaint. Only once did I hear either. An Illinois Lieutenant, as brave a fellow as ever drew a sword, had been shot through and through the thighs, fairly impaled by the bullet— the ugliest wound but one I ever saw. Eight days before, he weighed one hundred and sixty. Then, he could not have swung one hundred and twenty clear of the floor. He had just been brought over the mountain; his wounds were angry with fever; every motion was torture; they were lifting him as tenderly as they could; they let him slip and he fell, perhaps six inches. But it was like a dash from a precipice to him, and he wailed out like a little child, tears wet his pale, thin face, and he only said, "my poor child, how will they tell her?" It was only for an instant; his spirit and his frame stiffened up together, and with a half smile he said, "don't tell anybody, boys, that I made a fool of myself!" The Lieutenant "sleeps well," and alas, for the "poor child"—how did they tell her?

A soldier fairly riddled with bullets, like one of those battle-flags, lay on a blanket gasping for breath. "George," said a comrade and a friend before this cruel war began, with one arm swung up in a sling, and who was going home on furlough, "George, what shall I tell them at home for you?" "Tell them," said he, "that there isn't hardly enough left of me to say 'I,' but—hold down here a minute—tell Kate there is enough of me left to love her till I die." George got his furlough that night, and left the ranks forever. It seems to me that all true women must envy that girl's fate. Shot away all but his heart, that still beat true, who would not be the dead soldier's bride? Oh, there is nothing anywhere here to make you blush for human weakness; the bullet is not moulded that can kill Western manhood.

I want to say here, that the surgeons should be compelled to report to the WOMEN; if they do their duty, they have to perform in large measure woman's work. They need more than skill and scalpels; they want woman's fortitude, tenderness and faith. There are the noblest of men among the surgeons in the Army of the Cumberland, who do not halt at the letter of duty, but go on cheerfully to the spirit; and there are—GOD save the mark!—men among them for whom faithless is the mildest euphemism. I must tell one instance: a "contract" surgeon—if you know what that is—went out on a pleasure ride within the hour— three o'clock—that two hundred sick and wounded men came into his ward. He returned at sunset, and on being reminded of his neglected duty, flippantly replied, "Oh, I'll do them in half an hour!" What, think you, would "do" him and do him justice? For one, I should be quite content to trust his fate to the verdict of a jury of the women of the North, to whom be glory and honor everlasting!

WOMAN, THE SOLDIER'S FRIEND.

It is a white, dusty ridge in Alabama ; tall, slim oaks sprinkle it, and beneath them, in streets with a strange, far-eastern look, stand the tents of one of those blessed Cities of Mercy—a Field Hospital. The sun pours hotly down ; a distant drum snarls now and then, as if in a dream ; the tinkling concert of a cloud of locusts— the cicada of the South—comes, like the dear old sleigh-bells' chime, from a distant tree. "The loud laugh that tells the vacant mind" is unheard : the familiar sound of closing doors and children's carol never rises there ; the tents swell white and sad and still. Within them lie almost three thousand soldiers, marred with all wounds conceivable, wasted with pain, parched with fever, wearily turning, wearily waiting, to take up the blessed march. "Ho for the North !" That is the word, the ever-abiding charmer that "lingers still behind." It is Stevenson ; it is Nashville, it is Louisville ; it is home ; it is Heaven ! Alas, for it, how they falter and sleep by the way. And every one of these men was somebody's boy once ; had a mother once, a wife, a sister, a sweetheart, but "better is a friend that is near than a brother afar off," and now comes the blessed mission of women. True, there are only two here in person, but how many in heart and work!

You have been thinking, my sisters, where is *our* work in all these scenes? That snowy roll of linen; that little pillow beneath the sufferer's head; that soft fold across the gashed breast; that cooling drink the rude, kind, stalwart nurse is putting to yonder boy's white lips; that delicacy this poor fellow is just partaking of; that dressing-gown whose broidered hem those long, thin fingers are toying with; the slippers, a world too wide for the thin, faltering feet; the dish of fruit a left hand is slowly working at, his right laid upon our Federal altar at Chicamauga, never to be lifted more. *Your* tree, my sister, bore that fruit; *your* fingers wrought, your heart conceived. "What do the women say about us boys at home?" slowly asked a poor wreck of a lad, as I sat by his side. That brow of his ached, I know, for the touch of a loving hand, "and the sound of a voice that is still." At the moment he asked the question he was turning over a little silken needle-book that one of you laughing girls made one day, and tucked in a corner of a bag labeled "U. S. Sanitary Commission." On the cover of that book you had playfully wrought the words, "my bold soldier boy." I silently pointed to the legend; the reply struck home to his heart, and he burst into tears. I assure you they were not bitter tears he shed, and as he wiped them away with a white handkerchief you girls had hemmed for him, his question was twice answered and he was content. His eyelids closed down, his breathing grew regular; he had fallen asleep, and I thought it was the picture of the "Soldier's Dream" over again.

You hear of the malappropriation of your gifts, but never fear; one grain may fall, but two will spring up and blossom out into "forget-me-nots." Your work is everywhere. Go with me to that tent standing apart. It is the Dead-house tent. Four boys in their brown blankets, four whitewood coffins, four labels with four names on four still breasts. Two of the four garments the sleepers wear are of linen from your stores, stitched by your fingers. Verily, the Ladies' Soldiers' Aid Societies should be named "Mary," for are they not, like her of old, "last at the cross and earliest at the grave."

NIGHT RIDE OF THE WOUNDED BRIGADE.

"When can I go home, Doctor?" is the question forever shaped by the lips and asked by the eyes, as he goes his daily rounds. There was a train of cars at last—box cars—*cattle* cars, if you like it better—drawn up opposite the hospital, and I stood there on a bright

morning at nine o'clock, as the four hundred poor fellows, lame, bandaged, supported, carried outright, came
over the hill to take the train. It was the Wounded
Brigade, and three of every five wore some token of
woman's remembrance. It was announced to them the
night before that they were to go at five, and there was
no sleep for joy. Some of them had actually watched
the night out, in the open air, like the Chaldean shep-
herds, lest by some chance the train should go away
without them. But they were hopeful and heartful, for
they would go by-and-by. That Wounded Brigade
made my eyes dim as it came; no "pomp and circumstance" now; no martial step, no rustling banners, no
gleaming arms. I should have been less than human
had I not swallowed my heart all day as I thought of
that Brigade, the grandest body of men I ever saw in
my life. Well, the cars were *floored* with the sick and
wounded, and we moved slowly away, and I must tell
you that all along that weary ride of twenty hours to
Nashville, it was the thoughtful gift of woman that
kept their hearts up. Not on the field of Chicamauga,
not in the woods of Alabama, not on the train in Tennessee, could I get out of sight of the Aid Society, the
Sanitary Commission, the Florence Nightingales of the
North. I want to describe that ride; how the boys
went as *cattle* go, how they waited hours till a Major-

General's swift, commodious car should pass; how they crept along at the rear of everything alive.

If the mile-posts tell truth, there are one hundred and thirteen of them between the Field Hospital at Stevenson and the depot at Nashville, but if the train of the Wounded Brigade runs by honest time, there are four hundred.   When I saw the limping squadron trailing over the hill, a memory brightened into sight. It was of a Division drill, when the old-fashioned General—J. D. Morgan—sat away there upon his horse, and eight thousand men stood motionless on the field away here.   The sun glinted grandly from the hedges of bayonets, and the colors grew deep and rich in the light, and the breasts of dark blue were built into a wall. Now and then an aid galloped out from the group around the General, and down the line, and back to his position again.   The bugles blew, and the stately line was a column; a wing unfolded here and a wing there; they flapped together as noiselessly as an eagle's; it was in order of march; it was in line of battle, and the aids dashed out and the bugles blew on, and then the field was checkered with squares like a chess-board for a mighty game.   They were as true as a die; a mosaic of men; all exact as a page of Euclid; you looked and the evolution was complete.   There, in equal spaces between the angles of the squares, frowned a battery.

How it got there nobody could tell. In an instant
there was a glitter and a flash. The cavalry were upon
them! The outer rank to the knee; the next bent;
the next erect, and so the cones grew, quick as a turn
of the kaleidoscope—cones tipped with cold steel, and
the reflected light grew steady and still. There was a
rustle along the iron-clad porcupines; the batteries
disappeared; the hedges melted away, the squares were
columns, the columns were lines, and away marched
the battalions. And in all this there was no shout, no
oath, no loud command. The General away yonder
upon his horse moulded and fashioned the thousands at
will, as if he had been a sculptor modeling in clay, and
he was, and most masterly was the handling. He could
have taken them through Jerusalem's narrow gate, the
"Needle's Eye;" he could have poured them through
a defile like water. That handling of men is a rare art.
I have seen a Colonel make three attempts to get his
regiment through a fence gap two rails wide, and set it
to "*throwing*" the fence, at last, like a herd of unruly
cattle! Bullion on the shoulders of fools only makes
folly more conspicuous.

It was to that brilliant Division drill that my mind
swung back, when the Wounded Brigade hove in sight.
They were loaded upon the train; two platform cars
were paved with them, forty on a car. Seven boxes

were so packed you could not set your foot down among them as they lay. The roofs of the cars were tiled with them, and away we pounded, all day, all night, into the next morning, and then Nashville. Half of the men had not a shred of a blanket, and it rained steadily, pitilessly. What do you think of platform cars for a triumphal procession wherein to bear wounded heroes to the tune of "the soldier's return from the war?" Well, what I would come at is this: the stores of the Sanitary Commission and the gifts of women kept the boys' hearts up through all those weary, drizzling hours. It is midnight, and the attendants are going through the train with coffee graced with milk and sugar—think of that!—two fresh, white, crisp crackers apiece, and a little taste of fruit. Did your hands prepare it, dear lady? I hope so, for the little balance in your favor set down in the ledger of GOD But here they come with the coffee; will you go with them? Climb through that window into a car black as the Hole of Calcutta. But mind where you step; the floor is one layer deep with wounded soldiers. As you swing the lantern round, bandages show white and ghastly everywhere; bandages, bandages, and now and then a rusty spot of blood. What worn-out, faded faces look up at you. They rouse like wounded creatures hunted down to their lairs as you come. The tin cups extended in all sorts of hands but plump, strong ones, tinkle all around you. You are fairly girdled with a tin cup horizon. How the dull, faint faces brighten as those cups are filled! On we go, out at one window, in at another, stepping gingerly among mangled limbs. We reach the platform cars creaking with their drenched, chilled, bruised burdens, and I must tell you that one poor fellow among them lay with a tattered blanket pinned around him; he was literally *sans culotte!* "How is this?" I said. "Haven't got my descriptive list—that's what's the matter," was the reply. Double allowance all around to the occupants of the platforms, and we retraced our steps to the rear of the train. You should have heard the ghost of a cheer that rose and fluttered like a feeble bird, as we went back. It was the most touching vote of thanks ever offered; there was a little flash up of talk for a minute, and all subsided into silence and darkness again. Wearily wore the hours and heavily hammered the train. At intervals the guard traversed the roofs of the cars and pulled in the worn-out boys who had jarred down to the edges—pulled them in toward the middle of the cars without waking them! What a homeward march is all this to set a tune to!

By some error in apportionment there was not quite coffee enough for all on deck, and two slips of boys on

the roof of the car where I occupied a corner were left
without a drop. Whenever we stopped, and that was
two hours here and three hours there, waiting for this
and for that—there was no hurry—and the back door
was slided back in its groove, I saw two hungry faces
stretched down over the car's edge, and heard two feeble voices crying, "We have had nothing up here since
yesterday noon, we two—there are only us two boys—
please give us something. Haven't you got any hard-
tack?" I heard that pitiful appeal to the officers in
charge and saw those faces till they haunted me, and
to-day I remember those plaintive tones as if I were
hearing a dirge. I felt in my pockets and haversack for
a cracker, but found nothing. I really hated myself for
having eaten my dinner and not saved it for them. A
further search was rewarded with six crackers from the
Chicago Mechanical Bakery, and watching my chance
when Pete's back was turned—the cook a smutty auto-
crat was Pete in his way—I took a sly dip with a basin
into the coffee-boiler. As the car gave a lurch in the
right direction, I called from the window, "Boys!" I
heard them crawling to the edge, handed them up
the midnight supper, "Bully for you," they said, and I
saw them no more. When the train reached Nashville
and I clambered down to solid ground again, I looked
up at the roof; it was bare. And how do you like the
ride of the Wounded Brigade?

I do not write this in a censorious spirit. I do not
know but it was the best that could be done, yet I
thought—you cannot help thinking—that the passenger
train which left Stevenson with its load of civilians, sutlers, contractors and what-nots, at six dollars a man,
one hour before my poor Brigade, and pursued its way
"without let or hindrance," reaching Nashville thirteen
hours before it, could have had worthier occupants in
the persons of the boys in white bandages. I give it as
one of the pictures of war, just after the blossoming out
of a great battle. Men and women with tomb-stones
in their left breasts need it. Men and women who are
alive and warm deserve it that they may discern more
clearly the horrors they have alleviated. One truth you
ought not to forgive me should I fail to record ; during
all that day and night miserably craunched out between
wheel and rail, I did not hear one lisp or whisper of
complaint ! Are Federal soldiers gods or are they only
men ? Homer could have moved the machinery of his
Epic with them, and no thanks to Apollo "of the silver
bow."

After the Sunday's battle at Chicamauga, I heard a
young soldier who had been in   attles, and who was
holding a splintered arm as if it had been a pet baby,
lightly and laughingly talking of soldiers' hardships, and
there was neither grumble nor growl in the whole camp-

fire gossip. "Good government," said he, "of *course* it is. When we boys are at the North Pole and it wants us at the South, why it carries us in cattle cars, and we ride like gentlemen. But when we have only four or five hundred miles to go, why then it lets us *frog* it!" Among all the words born in camps, "skedaddle" and all, commend me to "*frog* it." It is as expressive as a picture.

"When I entered the service," he continued, "says they, 'why, you'll have a chance for three things if you enlist—study, travel and promotion.'" And so he rattled on, and a merry party they made of it.

How many noble women have threaded like rays of sunshine the heavy cloud of war, women of the nineteenth century fit to be named with Rachel and Ruth and Florence Nightingale. No better epitaph could be traced upon their tomb-stones than this:

"EACH SOLDIER'S SISTER AND EACH SUFFERER'S FRIEND."

As with the "Angel of the Crimea," so with them— the soldiers kissed the shadows that fell upon the pillows as they passed by. When the scenes amid which we wait and labor pass into the grand eternity of the historic page, the heart of the world will warm to the Women of the North; soldierly daring and womanly deeds will be blended forever; the kiss of the daughters will not stain the sword of the sons, and the lost Eden of old will smile once more on the map of the globe.

ARMY CHAPLAINS.

It would amuse you to see a man, almanac in hand, trying to find out the day of the month, and compelled to call·for aid at last. That thin day-book of time, if you have ever happened to think of it, presumes on your knowing one of two things, the day of the month or the day of the week. Ignorant of both, the almanac and the Koran are pretty nearly alike—sealed books. There is no place like the army for losing your reckoning; the days flow by in an unbroken stream; a month passes and you fancy it a fortnight, and it is no unusual thing to see a boy going about among his comrades hunting up the day of the week. The Sabbath, that sweetest blossom in the waste of time, is trampled by hurrying feet unnoted. It came and went yesterday and you find it out to-morrow. You are at sea, and though you may never have been a saint, yet when the Sundays keep dropping out of the calendar, so like withered leaves, it makes you somewhat uncomfortable for a sinner.

But how about the chaplains? you ask. I have
met three dozen men whose symbol is the cross, and of
that number, two should have been in the ranks, two
in the rear, one keeping the temperance pledge, one
obeying the third commandment—to be brief about it,
five repenting and eight getting common sense. The
rest were efficient, faithful men. Not one chaplain in
fifty, perhaps, lacks the paving-stones of good intentions, but the complex complaint that carries off the
greatest number is ignorance of human nature and
want of common sense. Four cardinal questions, I
think, will exhaust the qualifications for a chaplaincy:
Is he religiously fit? Is he physically fit? Is he
acquainted with the animal " man "? Does he possess
honest horse-sense? Let me give two or three illus-
trative pictures from life: Chaplain A. has a puttering
demon; he is forever not letting things alone. Passing
a group of boys, he hears one oath, stops short in his
boots, hurls a commandment at the author, hears
another and reproves it, receives a whole volley, and
retreats, pained and discomfited. Now, Mr. A. is a
good man, anxious to do duty, but that habit of his,
that darting about camp like a devil's darning needle
with a stereotype reproof in his eye and a pellet of
rebuke on the tip of his tongue, bolts every heart
against him. Chaplain B. preaches a sermon—regular

army fare, too—on Sunday, buttons his coat up snugly under his chin all the other days of the week, draws a thousand dollars, and is content. Chaplain C. never forgets that he is C., "with the rank of Captain," perfumes like a civet cat, never saw the inside of a dog-tent, never quite considered the rank and file fellow-beings. Of the three, the boys hate the first, despise the second, and d—n the third.

"Demoralize" has become about as common a thing in the army as a bayonet, though the boys do not always get the word right. One of them—"one of 'em" in a couple of senses—was talking of himself one night. "Maybe you wouldn't think it, but I used to be a regular, straight-laced sort of a fellow, but since I joined the army I have got damnably *decomposed!*" Now, a drunken General and a "decomposed" Chaplain are about as useless lumber as can cumber an army.

There is Chaplain D., well equipped with heart, but with no head "to speak of," and, with the purest intentions, a perfect provocative to evil. It was next to impossible for a man to put the best side out when he was by; a curious two-footed diachylon plaster, he drew everybody's infirmities to the surface. I think the regiment grew daily worse and worse, and where he was, words were sure to be the dirtiest, jokes the coarsest, deeds the most unseemly. The day before the battle of Chicamauga, the regiment had signed, almost to a man, a paper inviting him to resign, but on the days of the battles he threw off his coat and carried water to the men all day. In the hottest places there was Chaplain D., water here, water there, assisting the wounded, aiding the surgeons, a very minister of mercy. That 'invitation' lighted the fire under somebody's coffee kettle on Monday night. The Chaplain had struck the right vein at last; the boys had found something to respect and to love in him, and the clergyman's future usefulness was insured. The bond between Chaplain and men was sealed on that field with honest blood and will hold good until doomsday.

One noble Illinois chaplain, who died in the harness, used to go out at night, lantern in hand, among the blended heaps of the battle-field, and as he went, you could hear his clear, kind voice, "any wounded here?" and so he made the terrible rounds. That man was idolized in life and bewailed in death. Old Jacob Trout, a Chaplain of the Revolution, and who preached a five-minute sermon before the battle of Brandywine, was the type of the man that soldiers love to honor. His faith was in "the sword of the Lord and of Gideon," but his work was with the musket of Jacob Trout. I do not mean to say that the Chaplain should

step out from the little group of non-combatants that
belong to a regiment, but I do say that he must
establish one point of contact, quicken one throb of
kindred feeling between the men and himself, or his
vocation is as empty of all blessing and honor as the
old wine-flasks of Herculaneum. No man can mis-
understand what I have written. The chaplaincy, at
best, is an office difficult and thankless. It demands
the best men to fill it well and worthily, men whose
very presence and bearing put soldiers upon their
honor; and it is safe to say that he who is fit to be a
chaplain is fit to rule a people. How nobly many of
them have labored in the Army of the Cumberland!
Ministers of mercy, right-hand men of the surgeons
and the Nightingales, bearers of the cup of cold water
and the word of good cheer, the strong regiment may
be the Colonel's, but the Wounded Brigade is the
Chaplain's.

Writing of sermons, did you ever make one at a
field preaching at the Front? If not, I must give you
a homely little picture I saw yesterday, which by the
calendar was Sunday. Blundering past a rusty camp,
the tents stained and rent, I came upon a group of
about as many as met of old "in an upper chamber,"
and not an officer among them, unless it might be a
sergeant. They were seated upon logs, and the Chap-

lain was just leading off in a hymn, that floated up and
was lost, like a bird in a storm, amid the clash of bands
and the rumble of army wagons in the valley below.
The Chaplain wore a hat with a feather in it, that he
might have been born in, for any evidence I have to
the contrary, for during the entire services, praise, prayer
and preaching, the voice came out from beneath the
hat with a feather in it.   Perhaps it would have struck
you as irreverent, but it may be that he feared the mis-
fortune of the wolf who talked hoarsely with little Red
Riding Hood, because he had a cold in his head.   At
the heels of the Chaplain as he preached, a kettle was
bubbling over a fire, and a soldier-boy on his knees
beside it was apparently worshiping the hardware.
But he was no idolater for all that, since a closer look
discovered him fishing in it for something with a fork.
Around the preacher, but just out of sermon range,
boys were smoking, darning, chatting, reading, having
a frolic; the voice of a muleteer came distinctly up
from below, as he damned the hearts of his six in
hand—for no teamster I ever heard was so wild as to
swear at a mule's *soul;* the passing trains of ammunition crushed the Chaplain's sentences in two, and, now
and then, whistled a truant word away with them, but
he kept right on, clear, earnest, sensible—no matter for
the hat with a feather in it—and I could not help feel-

ing a profound respect for the preacher and the little group around his feet.

To mingle with the men, and share in their frolics as well as their sorrows, without losing self-respect; to be with them and yet not of them; to get at their hearts without letting them know it—these are indeed tasks most delicate and difficult, requiring a tact a man must be born with, and a good, honest sense that can never be derived from Gill's "body of divinity." "How do you like Chaplain S.?" I asked of a group of Illinois boys one day. "We'll *freeze* to him every time," was the characteristic reply, and not unanticipated, for I had seen him dressing a wound, helping out a blundering boy, whose fingers were all thumbs, with his letter to "the girl he left behind him," playing ball, running a race, as well as heard him making a prayer and preaching a sermon. The Surgeon and Chaplain are co-workers. I said the former should report to the Women, and I half believe that the Chaplain should do likewise.

THE SOLDIER'S "FIRST MAN."

Sharpshooting is the squirrel-hunting of war, and it is wonderful how utterly forgetful of self the marksmen grow; with what sportsman-like eyes they watch the grander game, and with what coolness and accuracy they bring it down. But indifferent as men become to human life, they have the most vivid and minute remembrance of the first man they brought down with a deliberate aim; often noting, in the instant of time preceding the fatal shot, the fashion of features, color of eyes and hair, even the expression of face, all painted in a picture that shall last the life out.

"My first man," said an artilleryman to me, "I saw but twenty seconds and shall remember him forever. I was standing by my gun, when an infantry soldier rushed up and made a lunge with the bayonet at one of the horses. I whipped out my revolver, took him through the breast, he threw up his hands, gave me the strangest look in the world and fell forward upon his face. He had blue eyes, brown, curling hair, a dark mustache and a handsome face."

The gunner paused a moment and added: "I thought the instant I shot that I should have *loved* that man had I known him. I tell you what—this war is terrible business." And so it is—and so it is— but "they that take the sword shall perish by the sword."

PAYMASTERS AND JEWELRY.

The coming of no officer, except a well-beloved commanding General, is so heartily welcomed by the boys, as that of those gilt-leafèd gentlemen with the iron trunks, the opening of which gives everything the color of spring, bringing the "green back" to the most withered prospect. An epitaph for a modern Paymaster can be easily stolen from Halleck's sweetest little poem, as thus:

"Green be the turf above him."

Just finishing the inscription, I read it and the explanation to a rough boy near by who was making jewelry. He looked up with, "Old Halleck write that?" "Fitz-Greene," said I. "That's what's the matter," said he, and worked away at his jewel again.

"Jewelry," you think and wonder, and perhaps it may be worth an explanation. The Tennessee and Stone rivers are strewn with shells of rare beauty and exquisite coloring; blue, green, pink and pure pearl. If you look in any boy's knapsack you will be quite sure to find a shell in it. Of these queer, broken, little chests of former life, the soldiers make rings, pins, hearts, arrows, chains, crosses; and to see the rough tools they use, and then note the elegance of form and finish in the things they make, would set the means and the results incredibly apart. With a flat stone for a polishing table, they grind down the shell, and then with knife and file shape little fancies that would not be out of place on a jeweler's velvet, and beautiful souvenirs of fields of battle. Every ring and heart has its bit of a story the maker is not reluctant to tell. This little touch of the fine arts gives to camps a pleasant, home-like look, and I have seen many a soldier putting the final polish to a pearl trinket by the light of his inch-of-candle flaring from a bayonet, as earnest over his work as if the shell possessed the charm of Aladdin's lamp, and rubbing it would summon spirits.

HEARING FROM HOME.

Occupation is a grand thing, and quite as important to the tone and heart of an army as hard bread and bacon. The monster against which Dr. Kane fought so successfully in the Arctic night, with theatre and frolic, wanders listlessly up and down the camps. Would you believe—and yet it is true—that many a poor fellow in the Army of the Cumberland has literally *died to go home;* died of the terrible, unsatisfied longing, home-sickness? That it lies at the heart of many a disease bearing a learned name? It is languor, debility, low fever, loss of appetite, sleeplessness, death, and yet, through all, it is only that sad thing they call Nostalgia. Who shall dare to say that the boy who "lays him down and dies," a-hungered and starving for home, does not fall as well and truly for his country's sake as if a bullet had found his heart out? Against it the surgeon combats in vain, for "who can minister to a mind diseased?"

The loved ones at home have something to answer for in this business, and it pains me to think that more than one man has let his life slip out of a grasp too weak to hold it, just because his dearest friends did not send him a prescription once a week, price three cents— a letter from home. Is some poor fellow sinking at heart because *you* do not write to him? If there is, lay my letter down at once and write your own, and may He who sent a messenger all the way from Heaven to earth with glad tidings, forgive you for deferring a hope to some soldier-boy. You would not wonder at my warmth had you seen that boy waiting and waiting, as I have, for one little word from somebody. Too proud to own, and yet too sincere to quite conceal it, he tries to strangle the thought of home, and goes into the battle, whence he never comes forth. An Indiana

soldier was struck in the breast at Chicamauga and fell.
The bullet's errand was about done when it reached
him; it pierced coat and underclothing, and there was
force enough left in it to wound if not to kill him. But
it had to work its way through a precious package of
nine letters, indited by one dear heart and traced by
one dear hand; that done, the bullet's power expended,
there it lay asleep against the soldier's breast! Have
you been making such a shield, dear lady, for anybody?
Take care that it does not lack one letter of being
bullet-proof.

THE NEW ENGLAND SCHOOLMA'AM.

The love for the old flag gushes out sometimes in the
most unexpected places like a spring in the desert, and
many a time have Federal prisoners been startled into
tears at finding a friendly heart beating close beside
them. A body of Federal prisoners had reached
Rome, Georgia, *en route* for Richmond. Weary,
famished, thirsting, they were herded like cattle in the
street under the burning sun, a public show. It was a
gala day in that modern Rome. The women mag-
nificently arrayed came out and pelted them with balls
of cotton, and with such sneers and taunts as, "So you

have come to Rome, have you, you Yankees? How
do you like your welcome?"—and then more cotton
and more words. The crowds and the hours came and
went, but the mockery did not intermit, and the poor
fellows were half out of heart. A Major, faint and ill,
had stepped back a pace or two and leaned against a
post, when he was lightly touched upon the arm. As
he looked around mentally nerving himself for some
more ingenious insult, a fine-looking, well-dressed boy
of twelve stood at his elbow, his frank face turned up
to the Major's. "And *he*, too?" thought the officer.

With a furtive glance at a guard who stood with his
back to them, the lad, pulling the Major's skirt, and
catching his breath boy-fashion, said, "Are you from
New England?" "I was born in Massachusetts," was
the reply. "So was my Mother," returned the boy,
brightening up; "she was a New England girl, and
she was what you call a 'school-ma'am' up North; she
married my father and I'm their boy, but how she *does*
love New England and the Yankees and the old
United States, and so do I!"

The Major was touched, as well he might be, and his
heart warmed to the boy as to a young brother, and he
took out his knife, severed a button from his coat, and
handed it to him for a remembrance. "Oh, I've got
half a dozen just like it. See here!" and he took from
his pocket a little string of gifts of other boys in blue.

" My mother would like to see you," he added, "and I'll go and tell her."

"What are you doing here?" growled the guard, suddenly wheeling round upon him, and the boy slipped away into the crowd and was gone. Half an hour elapsed and a lovely lady, accompanied by the little patriot, passed slowly down the sidewalk next to the curb-stone. She did not pause, she did not speak; if she smiled at all it was faintly; but she handed to one and another of the prisoners bank-notes as she went. As they neared the Major, the boy gave him a significant look, as much as to say, " that's my New England mother." The eyes of the elegant lady and the poor, weary officer met for an instant, and she passed away like a vision.

DRESSING FOR BATTLE.

When soldiers address themselves to battle, they generally go like men on business bound; the old blouse is good enough; the old hat will answer; they look to their guns a thought more critically; they tighten their belts a little, and they are ready. Officers seldom wear their finery into the field, the torn bars, the withered leaf the clipped eagle, the dim star, will do; but it is not always so. I have known a soldier make a most careful toilette on the eve of battle, attiring himself in his cleanest and best, as if he were going home. Perhaps the chance of such a thing may have drifted into mind; perhaps he had half a thought of anticipating the last hasty offices due the dead soldier; but I have been so often surprised out of my preconceived notions of what men are thinking who set forth to fight that I have ceased to entertain them altogether. General Grant is a quiet gentleman in a snuff-colored coat; Wood is twin-brother to his orderly; he went into battle in a shocking hat, a blouse "hutched up" like a Norwegian woman's boddice, and his pistol thrust in his belt like a whaler's knife; the commanding General hurled the Fourth Corps against Mission Ridge in a uniform too sleek and slippery for a young Lieutenant's callow · dignity. I know one General, however, who puts on his holiday apparel when he goes to battle. There is a glitter of buttons and stars where he is, and they were seen glancing like meteors at Stone River, Chicamauga and Mission Ridge, in the thick of the fight. "I want my men to know where I am," he said, adding with a smile, "and then those baubles light a man to danger and duty wonderfully well. He cannot decently *run* by star-light!" And there was something in the idea worth

thinking about. It puts a man upon his honor; we
somehow associate mean attire with mean actions, and
it is as easy to understand the feeling of the General as
of the great composer who, whenever he sat down to
dash off an immortal score, arrayed himself in the
garments wherein he appeared before the king.

SURVEYING ON HORSEBACK.

There are a thousand things about the preparations
for a battle that never challenge public admiration.
Among them is the topographical reconnoissance of the
enemy's country, involving slow science, quick movements, quicker wit, and the dash and courage of a
scout. Surveying on horseback and at a *quadrupe-
dante-pu* gait—in plain phrase, a smart Canterbury
gallop—is one of the achievements that would have
disturbed the polarity of the sober-going old compass-
bearers that were said to "run lines" when they only
meant they plodded them.

I have upon the drum-head under my eye—a bit of
parchment, by-the-way, upon which the long-roll has
been thrice beaten—a map of all the region round
about, from west of Mission Ridge to east of the
Chicamauga, and from Chattanooga to a point below

Crawfish Spring, an area of full forty miles. It is the work of a well known pioneer and civil engineer in the Northwest. In the immediate service of the commanding General, he is an improved edition of Cooper's "Pathfinder" escaped from the pages of the novelist. Think of a man's entering a farmhouse, demanding to see the title-deed of the owner, finding a "corner" therefrom, and then mounting his horse and dashing away, compass in hand, at the head of an escort of hard-riding dragoons, counting his horse's bounds as he goes, and so galloping along the line to the next "witness," as the surveyors name it. Think of his noting every feature of the surface, the woods, the fields, the hills, the vales, the distances, and delineating everything, till a map to fight by grows beneath his steady hand. Think of his doing all this, in forty-eight hours, in a region where bullets might swarm any minute like bees, and where they *did* fly like hornets. And this, incredible as it looks, is only the plain story in brief of an important service—one that has in it a dash of danger and romance that almost turns the loving needle into the flashing sword. This, at least: he "prospected" a region that proved as rich as any other region yet, in Federal valor and Federal blood.

OLD-TIME FORTS AND NEW.

There is hardly anything about the mechanism of war that so disappoints a civilian as his first glimpse of a modern fort. He thinks of towers and turrets and walls of stone; he sees a heap of reddish earth, tangled round the base with an ugly hedge of dry branches, and wrinkled with a deep trench. Wicker-work baskets—gabions, in military parlance—filled with earth, are ranged along the parapet; the smutty nose of a gun appears at breaks in the clay, here and there; he finds it fashioned like the crust of an immense chicken pie, though verily they that are in it are no chickens; a flagstaff, taken root in the hottest spot of the bare and trodden area, flaunts a flag; men lie asleep in the shadow of the wall; a solitary sentry paces to and fro, casting a glance at the landscape as he turns upon his heel. It is Fort Defiance or Albany or Ellsworth; it has a story; it has uttered a voice; it has been wrapped in a turban of cloud and thunder and thick lightnings; it has lashed a thousand men to the right about, but our civilian can hardly see how it all is. It has none of the pomp of war, and but precious little of the circumstance. The earth hereaway works as kindly into fortifications as the clay in the hands of the potter; much of it has a clear, red tint, and it will lie as you leave it, the jutting angle, the firm battlement, the smooth wall, with a look as finished as if it came from Paisley. Great masses of barren earth, where nothing grows but one strange flower that blossoms from a bare and barkless spar along the ramparts. And yet, homely and simple as it seems, nothing will so take the *vim* out of a shot as a heap of earth. It plunges into it—*thug*—and is dead. It is pounding dirt with hammers that forever fly off the handle. There are no splinters to impale you; a ball may sand your letter for you a little prematurely, but a few handy shovels will heal the wound in twenty minutes.

But there is a fort on the Potomac almost within bugle call of Mount Vernon that will gratify any little poetic sentiment this age of knocks may have left you: Fort Washington. It was there in 1812; for anything I can see it may be there in the twentieth century. Of hewn stone, time-stained, massive, angular, moss-grown, it looks like a castle in a picture. The parapet is dotted with guns in barbette; through the narrow embrasures in the walls below, looking like slits for air in a dungeon, you see muzzles of more guns in the casemates. Here are your demi-lunes and your bas-

tions, your sallyport, glacis and counterscarp, and your
everything that makes up a fine old figure in solid
geometry. You pant up the mountain path to the
grand entrance ; columns and capitals of stone are on
each side ; you cross a narrow bridge and come bolt
against a portcullis of a door made of massive timbers,
a door, as the song has it,

> "———as high as the sky,
> To let King George and his troops pass by,"

though no royal George ever did. In this ponderous
gate is a little door, something like Saint Peter's
wicket, that he opens to see who's there. You enter
and find yourself in an arched stone passage ; at your
right a wheel and chains ; above your head pulleys and
more chains. You begin to get the idea ; you are
standing, perhaps for the first time in your life, upon a
drawbridge, and you fumble in your memory for the
shout of some old castellan, " What, warder, ho ! down
with the portcullis ! Up with the drawbridge ! " The
wind draws cool through that arch of stone as if it
came from a sunless corridor. The sentinel presents
arms and you are out in the beaten area of the old
Fort. At your left and front are the balconied buildings of the officers' quarters, and beyond, those of the

men. You see the commandant, a fine, gray old Colonel, who looks as if he might be the very

> ————Colonel
> Who galloped through the white infernal
> Powder-cloud,"

in continental days.

You climb stone steps to the parapet; you visit
kennel after kennel of the surly dogs of war. You
mount the tower over the gateway; more dogs and a
sentinel, his bayonet as hot as a toasting-fork in the
sun. Descending, you pass dungeon-like doors going
to no end of mysterious cells for the villainous saltpetre; piles of solid shot resembling inverted clusters of
fabulous grapes. And what a splendid view you have
from the tower!—the ships and boats forever sliding up
and down, and the Potomac stretching away like an
arm of the sea, and the tide forever coming and going;
you stand out upon the bluff and gaze toward Mount
Vernon.

A FLASH OF SUNSHINE.

Now and then, a little human smile brightens war's
grim visage, like a flash of sunshine in an angry day.
The amenities of battle are so few, how precious they
become! Let me give you that little " touch of nature

that makes the whole world kin." The 3d Ohio,
belonging to Streight's command, entered a town *en
route* for Richmond, prisoners of war. Worn down,
famished, hearts heavy and haversacks light, they were
herded together, "like dumb, driven cattle," to wear
out the night. A rebel regiment, the 54th Virginia,
being camped near by, many of its men came strolling
about to see the sorry show of poor, supperless
Yankees. They did not stare long, but hastened away
to camp, and came streaming back with coffee-kettles,
corn bread and bacon—the best they had, and all they
had—and straightway little fires began to twinkle,
bacon was suffering the martyrdom of the Saint of the
Gridiron, and the aroma of coffee rose like the fragrant
cloud of a thank-offering. Loyal guests and rebel
hosts were mingled; our hungry boys ate and were
satisfied, and, for that one night, our common humanity
stood acquitted of the heavy charge of total depravity
with which it is blackened. Night and our boys
departed together; the prisoners in due time were
exchanged, and were encamped within rifle-shot of
Kelly's Ferry, on the bank of the Tennessee. But
often, around the camp-fires, I have heard them talk
of the 54th Virginia, that proved themselves so
immeasurably better "than a brother afar off:" heard
them wonder where they were, and discuss the chance

that they might ever meet. When they denounced the "damnable Johnny Rebs," the name of one regiment, you may be sure, was tucked away in a snug place, quite out of the range of hard words.

And now comes the sequel that makes a beautiful poem of the whole of it. On the day of the storming of Mission Ridge, among the prisoners was the 54th Virginia, and on the Friday following, it trailed away across the pontoon bridge and along the mountain road, nine miles to Kelly's Ferry. Arrived there, it settled upon the bank like bees, awaiting the boat. A week elapsed, and I followed suit. The Major of the 3d Ohio welcomed me to the hospitalites of his quarters, and almost the first thing he said was, "You should have been here last Friday; you missed the denoucment of that beautiful little drama of ours. Will you believe that the 54th Virginia has been here? Some of the boys were on duty at the Landing when it arrived. 'What regiment is this?' they asked, and when the reply was given, they started for camp like quarter-horses, and shouted as they rushed in and out among the smoky cones of the 'Sibleys,' 'the 54th Virginia is at the Ferry!' The camp swarmed in three minutes. Treasures of coffee, bacon, sugar, beef, preserved peaches, everything, were turned out 'in force,' and you may believe they went laden with plenty, at the double-quick to the Ferry."

The same old scene, and yet how strangely changed. The twinkling fires, the grateful incense, the hungry captives, but guests and hosts had changed places; the star-lit folds floated aloft for "the bonny blue flag;" a debt of honor was paid to the uttermost farthing. If they had a triumph of arms at Chattanooga, *hearts* were trumps at Kelly's Ferry. And there it was and then it was that horrid war smiled a human smile, and a grateful, gentle light flickered for a moment on the point of the bayonet.

A LITTLE PICTURE.

Even rough war has its bits of poetry, and to show how coarse and cheap materials may make a pretty picture, take the following: I was down on the bank of the Tennessee one bright day, and at my feet, with their square noses out of the water upon the rocky ledges, lay a school of pontoon boats, like a group of ungainly crocodiles. The architecture of one of those boats would give a yacht-fancier a fit of indigestion; of all the works of the ship-builder it is a menial donkey, with the proportions and finish of a watering-

trough. Busy about these boats were as hearty and
dirty a set of boys as ever fingered a rifle, and in each
boat was a stained rag of a dog-tent. Well, the order
came to move off up the river, sixteen miles, to Battle
Creek, where the pontoon bridge was to be laid down;
and the square noses backed off the rocks, one after
another; the dingy dog tents were bent on improvised
spars of red cedar, the old flag floated from the leading
boat in far-away mockery of the Admiral's flag-ship,
and so they slipped off, in a huddle at first, but
gradually streaming out and standing away, a fleet of
sixty sail. The dirty canvas grew clean in the sunshine; distance smoothed the rude boats; the red
woolen of the boys turned into the gay jackets of
gondoliers; they swept up to the bend of the river,
cutting the still shadows of the willows that fringed
the water, grew beautiful and strange and melted out
of sight.

The scene but an hour ago so full of life and noise
was silent; nothing audible but the stamping of the
horse that brought me there and the lapse of the lazy
water. A hawk far up in heaven floated slowly round
and round; across the river a thin spiral of smoke rose
above the trees; confiding in the stillness, a dappled
lizard glided along the log whereon I was seated,

scanning me with his curious jet bead of an eye, and as instinct with motion as a speckled trout.

It was a Southern noon in a Southern wilderness, the last boat had loitered out of sight, and I made my lonely way back through the woods, along the red ribbon of a road, stopped at a wayside well by a deserted cabin, and drew up the white, warped bucket by its rope of grapevine, glad of the creak of the parched windlass calling for water, and rode on till the rattle of the picket's piece made music and I was again at home within the living, bristling girdle of the old flag.

"DINNER TO THE FRONT."

The Front—syllable oftenest written, least under-stood—is an iron veneering mounted upon many legs. The moon's census reports nothing but a man. Life at the Front and life in the moon are alike. They are both worlds without women—such women as your mother and mine. The Front trails its kitchen after it like the train of a comet, and trundles its dinner across sovereign States.

If we cannot fight battles without powder, neither can we win them without pork; bread and bayonets go together, and so whatever pertains to an army's supplies possesses hardly less interest than the army itself. There is something upon the map to which the eye will turn quite as earnestly as to Chattanooga. It will be sure to trace that slender thread of communication drawn across two States, and to see in it the life-nerve of the Army. I give you a plain, unpainted deal box to bear with you to Chattanooga for the waiting boys. You shall go with it through a breadth of two hundred and fifty miles, where guerrillas range; shall cross three States and three great rivers; shall encounter a thousand perils and an hundred thousand foes who would care more to destroy that unpainted box than to save your soul alive. You shall be twelve days on the way, and the wonderful thing about the journey is that you reach your destination at all. The Chattanooga Railroad has grown historical. In its dilapidated, bullet-riddled cars, over the worn-out, ragged rails, hostile legions have fled and Federal columns moved on. These seats have sustained, in their turn, Bragg, Breckenridge and Johnston, Buell, Rosecrans and Grant. What victors and what vanquished, what burdens of hope and strength, what heavy freights of pain, what wounded and what dead have passed along those tattered bars of iron! And their office was never more important to Federal triumph than when over them went that plain deal box, not filled with jewels or medals of honor, but only with *hard bread*.

Night and day, day and night, forever to and fro, move the army wagons. If "England's morning drum beats round the world," the postillions' whips crack in ceaseless volleys from Nashville to Chattanooga. Think of an unbroken column of wagons two hundred and twenty miles long, rumbling over that bridge of boats across the Tennessee, as if the long roll were forever beating and remember that they bear the munitions of life, without which the munitions of war would be harmless as a drift of sand, and you feel that if the Front is formidable, the narrow bridge at Bridgeport, that can be swung round like a farm-yard gate, or trundled away upon wheels like quilting-frames, is vital to the well-being of the army. Nobody but a soldier can understand the difficulties of the tumbled-in and heaped-up world of mountains, nor the horrible gashes and torrent-beds called roads, over which our half-empty army-wagons have been knocking to pieces, or sinking below a wheelwright's resurrection. The mountain achievements of Hannibal and Bonaparte were trifles in comparison, and going over the ridges and through the clefts and up the craggy sides, the wonder grows, not so much how a vast army with ponderous artillery could ever have surmounted them,

as how, once over, it ever could have been main-
tained. Possibilities are suggestive. Take a time when
Chattanooga was a chicken-pie with the top off, and
the enemy looking down into it like the father of a
family at a Christmas dinner; looking down upon an
army one hundred and twenty-three miles from its base
of supplies by a single line of rail; the distance eked
out on thirty miles of river by three feeble little boats,
and finished off at last with nine miles of a mountain
road: a time when the 19th Illinois did duty upon
parched acorns; when the outlines of horses and mules
had their noses thrust in the morning feed of corn, and
were only sure of what they had in actual punishment
under the grinders, for soldiers would filch it away,
kernel by kernel—pick the stray grains out of the dirt,
to help on the hungry day. And this sharing of
rations was checked at last, for they locked up the corn
with a bayonet! A sentry paced before the noses of
the brutes, and mule and horse champed on unrobbed;
when many a soldier has picked a bone out of the
heap of offal, hidden it under his coat and slipped
away as if he had been a thief! And yet nobody was
starving.   It was only the shadow of a possibility
beginning to lengthen along the ground.

Why, here I have been riding a round hundred miles
to-day, and have had glimpses of the turnpikes all the

way, and everywhere have seen an unbroken line of
army wagons moving steadily toward Chattanooga,
winding down into the ravines, creeping up the
acclivities, drawing out into the little plains; and all
the while, another line moving toward Nashville, with
hardly a break in the stupendous procession. Arrived
at Murfreesboro, it was moving still. Advanced to
Stevenson, the head of the column is yet beyond. As
I saw the white canvas of the wagons through the
clouds of dust, I could liken them to nothing but a
thousand ants, each hastening away with its little white
grain of an egg. And all these tremendous arteries of
life, subsistence and ammunition, that meander a broad
State, constitute what Cæsar calls the *impedimenta* of
but a single grand army, whose victories are only
the results of marvelous combinations of machinery
gathered from all quarters, detailed, arranged and
converged by the sturdiest labors of thousands of men
whose names never appear in the brilliant dispatches
that flash over the whole land from commanding
Generals in the field. Stand beside a siege gun, a
hundred pounder, and you must be within musket
spatter of the enemy to know just how a man's heart
warms to those sturdy fellows that put in the pedal
base of a battle. Thirteen feet in length, a circum-
ference of seven feet at the breach and weighing ten

thousand pounds, it will toss a mass of iron without trying, as far as you can trot a sober pony in a round hour. It seems ponderous to be moved at all. Gravitation tugs at it as it tugs at the Cumberlands. Now attach to it the ten horses; set the broad mill wheels that bear it, deep in the ruts of a mortar-bed of a road; put the muscle of blue-shouldered wagoners to the wheel; heap the way before it with whole families of Bunyan's "Hill Difficulty," and then multiply that one gun by fifty, and set them all in motion, and you will begin to know how much it means when the General easily orders thunder and dinner for the Front.

'GETTING THE IDEA."

A sharpshooter at the battle of Chicamauga fancying General Granger to be game worth the powder, coolly tries his hand at him. The General hears the zip of the ball at one ear, but hardly minds it. In a minute away it sings at the other. He takes the hint, sweeps with his glass the direction whence the couple came, and brings up the marksman just drawing a bead upon him again. At that instant a Federal shot strikes the cool hunter and down he goes. That long range gun of his was captured, weighed twenty-four pounds, was telescope-mounted, and a sort of mongrel howitzer.

At one point there was a lull in the battle; at least it had gone shattering and thundering down the line, and the boys were as much "at ease" as boys can be upon whom any moment the storm may roll back again. To be sure, occasional shots and now and then a cometary shell kept them alive, but one of the boys ran down to a little spring, and towards the woods where the enemy lay, for water. He had just stooped and swung down his canteen, when *tick*—a rifle-ball struck it at an angle and bounded away. He looked around an instant, discovered nobody, thought it a chance shot—a piece of lead, you know, that goes at a killing rate without any malice prepense—and so, no-wise infirm of purpose, he again bent to get the water. *Ping*—a second bullet cut the cord of his canteen, and the boy got the idea; a sharpshooter was after him, and he went to the right-about and the double-quick to the ranks. The idea that he got might be pleasanter; when the notion that somebody is making a target of you creeps with its chilly feet slowly up your back, you can hardly help shrinking into yourself, though you may not be quite ready to own it.

A division surgeon was riding across a field where the battle had raged fiercely but just swept on, and was making his way slowly among the drifts of friends and foes—the blue and the gray together—when a wounded Federal soldier asked for water. The surgeon gave him the draught, when a voice from a gray heap near by said, "Won't you give *me* one too, Doctor?" "Certainly I will," and he was just raising the soldier and bringing round the canteen slung under his arm to put it to his lips when a cannon shot from a hostile battery struck the earth on one side; a second bounded by on the other. The man looked up in the surgeon's face with a half smile, "I am afraid they mean *us*, Doctor." At that instant, a third shot hit the target, and a headless trunk fell from the supporting arm.

Soldiers own to little fear of shells unless they come in a swarm. They are great, droning, humdrum humble-bees, and go to the tune of "get out of the way," but your miserable little pellets of lead—zip and thug out of the cedars! Shell are queerly behaved things, often harmless against all probabilities, and when you would think they must be deadly, only hatching thunder. If a shell passes you by only a few feet before it bursts, you are pretty sure to be good for the next one that comes, since each fragment takes its share of the motion and flies on. If a shell shows symptoms of making a landing just in front of you, your best route would seem to be towards and past the shell, but how rapidly one could run in that direction I have no means of knowing, never having seen the man that tried it. A solid shot is the most deceptive of projectiles. It may seem to move lazily, to be almost dead, but so long as it moves at all beware of it. Just before the battle, an artilleryman received his discharge for disability, but delaying for some reason his northward journey, he was yet with his battery on the eve of the engagement, and true to his instincts took his old place beside his horse, and was just preparing to mount when a solid shot came ricochetting across the field, bounded up and struck him in the lower part of the body. Crying out, "I've got the first ticket, boys," he sank down and only added, with that strange dread of a *little* hurt a terribly wounded man almost always seems to feel, "lay me by a tree where they wont run over me." They complied with his request, hastened into position, and saw him no more. The poor fellow's discharge was confirmed by Heaven. Now, that fatal ball, when, having finished its work there, it leaped lazily on, pushed out the skirt of the artillerist's coat as a hand would move a curtain, without rending it!

A MEDAL STRUCK IN THE SKY.

The night after the battle of Mission Ridge an officer
had gone in pursuit of the flying enemy and met with a
sharp resistance near Chicamauga Station, some two
miles beyond the Ridge.

At about seven o'clock on that November evening,
he sent a regiment to take possession of a little promontory jutting out into the valley, which would give
him a vast advantage. The musketry were briskly
playing all the while, time was precious, the position
important, the regiment a long time executing the
movement, and the commander, anxious and impatient,
was watching the sky line to see the troops emerge
from the shadows and move along the clear-cut crest of
the promontory. The moon, then near the full, had
just risen above the edge of the hill, when the
battalions moved out of the darkness and exactly
across the moon's disc. There for an instant was the
regiment, colors and gleaming arms in bold relief and
motionless; a regiment transferred to heaven! And
there was the moon, a great medallion struck in the
twinkling of an eye, as if in honor of that deathless

day.   The General's eye brightened at the sight. Even there it was something to be thought of; to be seen but a moment; to be remembered forever.

"SMALL DEER."

Rats, flies—the old-fashioned brown house-fly—and —well, you know what Burns spied on a lady's bonnet, and so, in his

"Oh, wad some power the giftie gie us,"

endowed it with immortality—all follow the army. They are everywhere.   The last named creature, against which care and cleanliness are no adequate defense, is a superior production.   Equip a kernel of half-macerated wheat with a small detail of legs—say six or eight—a mouth and an appetite, and then draw a modest gray stripe along its back, and you have the famous "gray-back," the crowning entomological triumph of the army.   It has no more respect for the "deeply, darkly, beautifully blue" of the officers than it has for the ragged blouse of the men.   Tenacious of life and woolen shirts, it thrives in water at any less temperature than 212 degrees, Fahrenheit, and the only use made of its belongings is to throw the name it bears at the next meanest creature encountered in these regions. Now the rats, the flies, and the gray-backs are blessings! The two former are nature's licensed scavengers and deserve protection. Consider the camp offices they perform, and you will leave them unharmed; and as for the gray-backs, they furnish most uneasy and intolerable arguments for personal cleanliness, and a single gray-back has driven a soldier to soap and water who could hardly have been persuaded thither by a bayonet.

I saw this morning a squad of the pioneer corps, with the train of led mules, each one having managed to creep under a pair of immense willow panniers, and to get upon his legs, the handles of spades, pickaxes and shovels bristling from the tops of the panniers like the shafts of arrows from the quiver of Apollo.

The impression you gain from looking at any one mule, is of a very lean rat under a couple of clothes-baskets—such as Falstaff got into, if we can credit Shakespeare—but the whole train winding its way among the mountains, the little emblem X of crossed axes glittering on the blue sleeves of the pioneers, suggests a scene in the Orient, and has not the least of an American look. The mule is an "institution;" dead or alive, he is everywhere; he trails the great banging wagons up mountains and down ravines where cavalry can hardly ride; of the six-mule power and the musketry of the postillion's whip you never get out of sight and hearing. If the wagon—of the exaggerated Pennsylvania species—gets the better of brake and chain, and goes hammering itself to pieces down a rocky path that nothing ever went down before but a crazy torrent, the driver adroitly throws his rear team, chucks them under the wheels, and brings everything to a jingling, crashing halt. No wonder the mule brays in its rusty way—the only creature extant that can slip all its misery to the tip of its tongue. I only wonder it does not pray. Its tail a miserable wisp, its mane a worn-out shoe brush, its ears "the chief end" of it, the mule is about as much an artificial production as a wooden nutmeg; and yet no steed from Barbary ever had a foot so beautiful. And yet, without the creature to which a thistle is a treat, the battle of Mission Ridge could never have been won.

ARMY PETS.

They have the strangest pets in the army, that nobody would dream of "taking to" at home, and yet they are little touches of the gentler nature that give you some such cordial feeling when you see them, as there is in the clasp of a friendly hand. Observation attests that the tenderest care for suffering comrades does not come from the recruit fresh from home and its endearments, but from the rough, battle-worn, generous fellows to whom they are only a long cherished memory. One of the boys has carried a red squirrel "through thick and thin" over a thousand miles. "Bun" eats hard-tack like a veteran, and has the freedom of the tent. Another's affections overflow upon a slow-winking, unspeculative little owl, captured in Arkansas, and bearing a name with a classical smack to it—Minerva. A third gives his heart to a young Cumberland Mountain bear. But chief among camp pets are dogs. Riding on the saddle-bow, tucked into a baggage-wagon, mounted on a knapsack, growling under a gun, are dogs brought to a premature end as to ears and tails, and yellow at that; pug-nosed, square-headed brutes, sleek terriers, delicate morsels of spaniels, "Tray, Blanche, Sweetheart, little dogs and all." A dog, like a horse, comes to love the rattle and crash of musket and cannon. There is one in an Illinois regiment, and, I think, regarded as belonging to it, though his name may not be on the muster-roll, that chases half-spent shot as a kitten frolics with a ball of worsted. He has been under fire and twice wounded, and left the tip of his tail at the battle of Stone River. Woe to the man that shall wantonly kill

him. But I was especially interested in the fortunes
of a little white spaniel that messed with a battery and
delighted in the name of " Dot." No matter what was
up, that fellow's silken coat must be washed every day,
and there was need of it, for when the battery was on
the march they just plunged him into the sponge-
bucket — not the tidiest chamber imaginable — that
swings like its more peaceful cousin, the tar-bucket,
under the rear axle of the gun-carriage—plumped him
into that, clapped on the cover, and Dot was good for
an inside passage. One day the battery crossed a
stream and the water came well up to the guns.
Nobody thought of Dot, and when all across, a gunner
looked into the bucket; it was full of water and Dot
was as dead as a little, dirty door-mat. Departed,
mourned and buried, it is time to put a dot to his
story.

All about the camps—the wildest and roughest of
them—you cannot get out of sight of the one touch
of nature. Thus, reared aloft on a single stilt, through
the camp whence I am now writing, you may see neat,
snug cottages for the Martin family, that despite war
and high prices, yet wear the rich satin of the old-time.
I close my eyes, a moment, and their pleasant talk, as
they sit upon their balconies, bears me, like the song
of a dear, dead singer, back to the homes afar and the
days that are no more.

A FLAG OF TRUCE.

Did you ever go out with a flag of truce? If not, let me give you a touch of a new experience. A group of horsemen approach our pickets with a white flag. They are halted, wheeled about, their backs to the Federal lines, their rank demanded, and a messenger dispatched to headquarters announcing the arrival and asking if the flag will be received. If disposed to grant an interview, a Federal officer of equal rank with the bearer of the message is sent out, and, if fortunate, you accompany him. As you ride up, it surprises you a little to see each salute the flag; surprises you more to see that they shake hands and smile like old friends; surprises you most when a Confederate officer produces a bottle of wine and challenges his *vis-a-vis* to a stirrup-cup. The officers bearing and receiving the message dismount, move apart and confer. The errand may be to pass a lady through our lines to the North, or to propose a four-and-twenty hours' armistice, or to play a card or two in the game of Bragg. The little aside conference over, the groups meet and mingle on that hand's breadth of neutral ground, spend a few moments in conversation, apparently free and frank, salute each other and wheel away, returning each to his own. The white flags have hardly flickered out of sight, when, blow, great guns! Lookout may growl, and Moccasin Point crack a fiery whip. While the interview lasts, the opposing pickets lean upon their muskets and look on. Dark-blue clusters watch it from the parapets of the forts in sight, and the butternut and gray enemy crawl out from their rifle-pits and look on, too. It is a grateful breathing spell for all colors.

Flags of truce and the bearing of hostile pickets toward each other always puzzle a civilian. He cannot imagine how men can stand front to front that may turn upon each other any hour, even as the upper and nether mill-stones, and grind out life and heart like grain, and not bear, man to man, the deadliest hate. And yet nothing can be further from the truth. Right on the eve of the battle Federal pickets contentedly munch biscuit that their neighbors-in-law have tossed to them; and an examination of many a plug of the Indian weed in a picket's pocket would show the print of a rebel's teeth at one end, and a "Yankee's" at the other.

The small currency of gibe and joke passes as freely among them as it does around a steamboat landing in the "piping times of peace," and I half fancied that a sort of rough, rude friendship might have sprung up among some of them. On Monday, the day of our reconnoissance in force at Mission Ridge, when the Federal skirmish line moved out, the hostile pickets stood and looked wonderingly upon it, and not till our advancing line was tipped with fire did they get the idea that serious work, work with blood and death in it, was actually beginning.

No elbow pagans in a little village at the hateful age of gossip, who divine each other's breakfast by the smell of the kitchen smokes, ever knew more of their neighbors' business than the troops on Mission Ridge and Lookout seemed to know of ours. On Sunday night, before the battle, rations of hard-tack and eighty rounds of ammunition had been issued. That very Sunday night, an Indiana regiment went out to picket duty, and the first salutation from the rebel line was, "Ho, ho! you Yanks think of fighting, do you? Got eighty rounds, did you, and hard bread to match!" There were five thousand men in Chattanooga at that moment, to whom it would have been the freshest of news. Two hostile armies may be wonderfully intimate.

A RIVER ROUTE IN WAR TIME.

I used to wonder at an eccentric old father who
named his daughter " Tennessee," but now I can understand and pardon the strange conceit, for it is, indeed,
a beautiful thing that girl was named for.   The
steamers that navigate the Tennessee are not gems of
naval architecture; the gilded saloons are "in the
mind's eye;" the state-rooms are in a state of nature;
the whole craft is scow-y to a degree and dangerously
dirty, and yet neither Cleopatra nor the Doge of Venice
ever floated in barge so graceful as the "Paint Rock".
seemed to me before the battle of Mission Ridge. To
be sure, she sat on the river like a tub, but in my eyes
she "walked the waters like a thing of life."   The last
throw of the locomotive dice-boxes has tumbled you
out at Bridgeport within an ace of your life, and con-
cluding to take to the water, you make for a tall smoke
under the river bank, and slide down a slippery path,
in a turbulent current of box and barrel.   Beside you,
swaying like the tethered elephant in the menagerie, is
a broad-nosed, amphibious-looking creature, apparently
built around a very quaint and greasy engine, while
you can hardly persuade yourself that the chimneys

were not set up on end and thrust above the tree-tops simply because there was no room for them below. On the edges around this engine are masses of blue, thinly sprinkled with sutlers and contractors. Here and there a gentleman in black, with a haversack blacker still, represents the Christian Commission.

You pick your way amid box and bale to the upper deck, with its warped and creaking floor, and the cabin is before you; a flapping canvas reared on the slenderest of umbrella frames, and looking like the tent of a side-show. Within is neither fire nor light nor seat. You plump down incontinently upon the floor, produce a candle and a sandwich from your knapsack, button up your coat, and there you are, a first-class passenger. The aguish steamer moans; the solemn trees begin to glide along the river banks; you are under way, and so giving your blanket a wisp you fall asleep, and make a night of it. In the gray of the morning you look out, and to your delight the steamer lies with its nose to the shore, and Bridgeport in plain sight. You have been waiting for the fog to lift; you have not gone a mile! Starved with hunger and cold you get under the lee of a log cabin, two stories high, built up square and strong in the middle of the deck, and discovering that it is the bullet-proof pilot-house you catch yourself wishing you had a lease of it.

Little bells tinkle, big bells clang, there is a rush of steam, the great wheel, hung on behind, like a reel at the stern of an emigrant's wagon, because there was no room for it aboard, begins to turn slow, and the craft swings shoreward, just abreast of a garden, to wood up. A couple of dozen negroes stream duskily out from the lower deck, and the garden fence of red cedar is shipped in ten minutes, leaving not a rail or a wreck behind; innocent onions and infant cabbages, every esculent and succulent of them all, left to the tendei mercies of hungry pigs and the cold world. Bang goes the bell, the hungry fires lick up the sweet morsels of cedar, the engine gives great sighs of content, we push bravely against the current, and such is "wooding up" on the Tennessee.

THE DEVIL'S COFFEE MILL.

Did you ever see one of the Devil's Coffee-mills? I saw ten of them to-day, like the immemorial black-birds, "all in a row,"—the "Union Repeating Gun" —an implement that might do tremendous execution in skirmishing were it not as liable to get out of order as a lady's watch. Imagine a big rifle mounted upon a light pair of wheels, and swung easily upon an arc

of a circle by a lever under the gunner's left arm so as
to sweep the enemy like a broom. Fancy a coffee-mill
hopper where the lock ought to be, and a crank to
match. Then here is a little copper box fitting the
hopper. You fill it with a dozen or twenty cartridges,
clap it into the hopper, and the thing is ready for
business. The gunner seats himself comfortably
behind the gun, elevates or depresses it with a touch,
and takes sight. Before his face as he sits, and
attached to the gun-barrel, is a steel shield about the
shape of an overgrown shovel and inclined a little
towards the miller, so that a shot aimed affectionately
at his head glances up and flies harmlessly away.
Through the center of this shield is a narrow slit—*a la*
Monitor-turret—which enables him to take sight.

Now, all things ready, the diabolical grist of bullets
in the hopper, the gunner—if he is a gunner—with the
rudder under his left arm, turns the crank with his
right hand, and the play begins. I saw one of them
work; it was tick, tick, tick, sixty to the minute, as
fast as you could think; no brisk little French clock
ever beat faster. When the barrel gets hot, there is
another in that chest; when the grists are all out and
the battle over, you pack the whole affair in a sort of
traveling-trunk, slip in a pair of shafts, with a horse
between them, in a twinkling, and trundle it off as

lightly as the cart of a bowery butcher-boy. But
soldiers do not fancy it. Even if it were not liable to
derangement, it is so foreign to the old, familiar action
of battle—that sitting behind a steel blinder and
turning a crank—that enthusiasm dies out; there is no
play to the pulses; it does not seem like soldiers' work.
Indeed, they regard it much as your genuine man-of-
war's man is apt to look upon the creeping, low-lying
mud turtles of Monitors, when, shut up in an iron box,
he remembers with a sigh the free decks and upper air
broadsides of his dear, old, stately ship-of-the-line,
whose "fore-foot" lifts grandly on the waves as if she
were going up a sea-green stairway, and who shakes
her splendid plumage as if she were ready to fly.

•

FATIGUE

How slow we are to learn that a battle is only the
apex of a pyramid it has worn out thousands to build;
the apex on which the sun streams a single ray of
glory, while all the rest is lost in the shadows below.
As I write, bodies of cavalry and baggage-wagons
and pontoon trains are moving by, eight days from
Nashville over the mountains, each whiff of hot air
hatching a trooper out of the yellow cloud of dust, not

a discernible trace of uniform, and ready to throw himself upon a couple of fence rails laid side by side, mutter thanks, as Sancho Panza did, to the man who invented sleep, and fall out of conscious existence in a twinkling and make no sig

On one occasion, when Roddy and Forrest, with five thousand men, were hard after Streight, a halt was ordered for an hour's rest. The boys rolled from their saddles into the bed of dust beside their horses' feet, and were asleep in a minute; a slumber so nearly own brother to death that the hour elapsed, the trumpet could not waken them, and the officers had actually to shake each man as he lay, and that, too, in a hostile land and a strong, swift enemy behind him. This is fatigue in its fullest sense, and, if you will multiply that trooper by eighty thousand, and parch him with thirst and set him on his feet in the burning dust, and bid him take his life in his hands and march and watch and fight until the burden of his thought is, "just one wink of sleep," that would be unbroken by the spatter of muskets and the growl of great guns, possibly you ·vill have an approximate idea of what it is to be fatigued.

THE LITTLE ORDERLY.

You remember the story of little Johnny Clem, the atom of a drummer-boy, " aged ten," who strayed away from Newark, Ohio, and the first we know of him, though small enough to live in a drum, was beating the long roll for the 22d Michigan. At Chicamauga, he filled the office of a " marker," carrying the guidon whereby they form the lines, a duty having its counterpart in the surveyor's more peaceful calling in the flagman who flutters the red signal along the metes and bounds. On the Sunday of the battle, the little fellow's occupation gone, he picked up a gun that had slipped from some dying hand, provided himself with ammunition, and began putting in the periods quite on his own account, blazing away close to the ground, like a fire-fly in the grass. Late in the waning day, the waif left almost alone in the whirl of the battle, one of Longstreet's Colonels dashed up, and, looking down at him, ordered him to surrender: " Surrender!" he shouted, "you little d—d son of a ——!" The words were hardly out of the officer's mouth, when Johnny brought his piece to " order arms," and as his hand slipped down to the hammer he pressed it back, swung up the gun to the position of "charge bayonet," and as the officer raised his sabre to strike the piece aside, the glancing barrel lifted into range, and the proud Colonel tumbled dead from his horse, his lips fresh stained with the syllable of reproach he had hurled at the child.

A few swift moments ticked off by musket shots, and the tiny gunner was swept up at a swoop and borne away a prisoner. Soldiers, bigger but not better, were taken with him, only to be washed back again by a surge of Federal troopers, and the prisoner of thirty minutes was again John Clem "of ours," and General Rosecrans made him a Sergeant, and the stripes of rank covered him all over like a mouse in a harness, and the daughter of Mr. Secretary Chase presented him a silver medal appropriately inscribed, which he worthily wears, a royal order of honor, upon his left breast, and all men conspire to spoil him, but, since few ladies can get at him here, perhaps he may be saved. Think of a sixty-three pound Sergeant, fancy a handful of a hero, and then read the "Arabian Nights" and believe them.

NASHVILLE STREET SCENES.

The scene is strange enough to have been born of a heavy supper at midnight. Tented towns where rose spacious and elegant homes; red, trodden earth where landscape gardens undulated; the old households scattered and gone; the old home charm departed; the stranger within the gates. One incessant, turbulent stream rolls through the streets all day long. Through tangles of all-colored humanity, from Congo to Christendom, meeting now the Beauty and now the Beast, you make your way. As far as you can see, army wagons raised to six-mule power; now ambitious barrels mounted upon two wheels borne along in the current; a wave of cavalry swelling the tide; stars, single and double, glittering on the top of the stream, and spread eagles floating, and silver leaves drifting on in pairs; now in an eddy at a corner, whirl ponderous artillery and little Africans, ambulances and ammunition, bread and bayonets. Horsemen tack their way on, doubling a cape of mules' ears, beating up in the lee of a school of caissons, astern of a baggage wagon; orderlies dash by at a gallop, while soldiers make a dive into the channel, dart like trout among hoofs, wheels and noses, and come up safely on the other shore.

The city pulsates like a heart with regiments moving to the Front. Depots are congested, trains show blue like full veins, sidewalks are azure, hotels cerulean, but not heavenly. You see, linked in the same train, cars labeled " Memphis," " Charleston," " New Orleans," " Indianapolis," " Galena and Chicago," " Michigan Southern "—a perfect pentecost of railroads—and such a train. Next to the engine is a block-house on wheels, bullet-proof, and filled with armed soldiers, the effect of the whole, with its broad ungainly front, being that of an anomalous " bull-head."

There is a blue elbow angling in each side, and a regulation shoe planted exactly across your single file of toes, and there seems to be no place for you any-where, and you begin to see that while " the pen is mightier than the sword " is all very well in the play and among the Scribes, it is very far from being true in a wide-awake department of the army, where the scale of being runs downward thus: men, munitions, mules, scribblers; brigades, batteries, bacon, beasts, Bohemians. But everybody knows that despite the absurd declama-tion of a very few officers against the press as a power in time of war, the work of the army correspondents was worth tons of powder to the Federal hosts, while of those who denounced the press so wildly it may be justly said, " nations could be saved without them."

The first thing in the street scenes that startles you with a loud knock at the left breast is this: in the endless procession of army trains comes a two-horse, canvas-covered wagon, with very much the look of the noisy vehicles that churn pure country milk over city pavements. You cannot tell why you looked at it at all, but, as you did so, you saw lashed to its side a device something like a bier— two parallel shafts connected by a piece of sacking. In the rear of the wagon, on each side of the door, the end of a keg was visible, neatly fitted into place. It needed nobody to tell you it was your first glimpse of an ambulance—the flying hospital—that, with its burdens of anguish and death, moves to and fro upon the field of blood. Like the flag of truce—that most beautiful emblem in the world—the ambulance should be free of all fields. One passed you a minute ago, labeled " 805," and the figures are as solemn as the Dead March in Saul. You may make a charge without flinching, when the heart beats the long roll like a drum, but to enter the terrible storm again and again with an ambulance, and assist to place tenderly within it its freight of agony, calls for the coolest courage and the firmest resolution.

You see the undertakers jostling the vanities· to gain a glance of your eye; the undertaker, who of all tradesmen succeeds in his undertaking, and whose work once done for you is done "for good and all." The embalmers, too, elbow each other and wrangle over their coffins as to which you shall lie down in. One exhibits a dog in a glass case, upon which he has tried his art preservative; he declares it a triumph, for though the bark is gone the body remains. Coffins stand up on end, empty and hungry, and petition you to get in and be composed; a transparency suggests that you be embalmed; a lantern persuades you to go to the "Varieties." You see, standing here and there, oblong, unpainted boxes, awaiting shipment, with the word, "head" written upon one end, and you shall think, as I do, "Yes, there is where he fell—in the front, at the head of the army."

But the sad scenes daily witnessed in their rooms make you forget the strange rivalry of the undertakers; mothers and wives with tear-stained faces waiting there for the dear, dead boy and love they would save, just a *little* longer, from the sweeping yet merciful sentence, "to dust shalt thou return." Old fathers, tremulous and yet content, for the agony of suspense is over, and the soldier "sleeps well," are waiting to bear the silent

burdens back to the homes they left so brave and
strong.

Amid these whirls and eddies of intensest life and
wildest death, you encounter something every day that
might have walked forth from an unbolted tomb, or
stepped out of a tarnished old picture frame of a
hundred years ago.   Wagons, rickety and ribbed,
resembling so many scows worn down to skin and
bone, creep painfully into town, drawn by two horses
tied up with ropes and strings, and tapered out with a
third ; wagons filled with the nursing mothers of Africa,
the ragged children of Ham and various " truck."   It is
a picture " toted " straight out of the Old Dominion,
the visible symbol of a plantation break-down.   Look
at that wheel, its rim guiltless of any iron ; there,
before your eyes, are the meaning and burden of the
song,

"Old Virginny never tires!"

Sometimes you see old-world mourners, the black
crape streaming out broadly from their hats behind,
and slowly turning to larboard and starboard like a
rudder, as they walk.   The old gentlemen of the ruffled bosoms—so ruffled and yet so placid !—you might
have seen a dozen years ago on the shady side in the
morning, looking as if they had stepped out of a dim
and ancient picture into life and light again, have

disappeared. You see old hand-organs, in the green baize petticoats, grinding out, in the midst of phthisicky gasps, the grist of tunes taken to the mill "when cats wore fillets." But when a swarthy fellow plants a monstrous quadrant before your quarters, and begins to vex the nerves of what proves to be a harp old enough to have been King David's, and to sing about "der Rhein" in a voice that, like Paul's, would "almost persuade you to be a Christian" and escape to Heaven and be out of hearing, you half suspect there must have been a partial resurrection.

You ask for the young men of Nashville; the high-spirited, delicately-nurtured sons. They are not here. They are sleeping on many a battle-field all over the South; they have perished. Nay, look over yonder, on the slope below the weeping willows; that field checked with little white head-boards is full of them. You walk along the streets sweet with the white blossoms of the Magnolia tree, and you will see the tokens of black crape poured out like a grief from between the closed blinds, and hundreds of the women of Nashville clad in mourning for the misguided dead. You meet them everywhere, and a feeling made up of sadness and loneliness comes over you as you think of these circles scattered and stricken forever for a worthless sake. I shall never be done admiring the patriotic devotion of the loyal women of the land, but I must tell you that the women of the South are worthy, in everything but a sacred cause, of their Northern sisters. There is nothing they will not surrender with a smile; the gemmed ring, the diamond bracelet, the rich wardrobe. They cut up the rich carpets for soldiers' blankets without a sigh; they take the fine linen from their persons for bandages. In all there is a defiant air, a pride in their humility strange to see. Of a truth they carry it off grandly. And almost all are in mourning for the dead brothers, lovers, friends, whom they had smiled into the army and driven into rebellion, and who have billowed all the South with their graves.

A HINT OF DESOLATION.

All the region around Chattanooga is so rich in caves that it seems almost invested in a cellular tissue. You find them in unexpected places. Remove the little wash of earth at the base of a ledge and there yawns a cell, the entrance worn smooth by unknown feet in some forgotten time. In the sides of the mountains are caverns, often of great extent, and yet waiting the torch of the explorer. Lookout has two; to one of them a large number of women and children fled for refuge, on the approach of the swarm from the Yankees' northern hive, and there some of them are said to have died. This is of so great extent, and works its way into the gloom by passages so numerous and uncertain, as if it would feel out the secret of the mountain, that although adventurous boys—and what will they not dare to do!—have groped their way into it, yet its recesses remain a mystery. Some of these caves have figured in the story of the rebellion, from the "villainous saltpetre" they supplied. Others, within a half hour's stroll of the heart of Chattanooga, that have evidently failed to awaken the lazy indifference of the former residents, had they been within Yankee reach would have been long ago explored and christened, had their little legends, and borne upon their rocky lintels the names of many a pair of pilgrims.

I visited one, where, perhaps a month ago, a discovery was made, that anywhere else but in the Front would have been a nine-days' wonder. Here it survived nine minutes. The entrance to the cave is abrupt, and a tree trunk had been thrust down, perhaps by a curious Indian of the tribe of John Ross that once ranged those lovely valleys and raised "a far cry" from the summit of Mission Ridge; thrust down so

long ago, that a dendrologist—a tough word for a
writer of plain English—would be puzzled to class it.
Well, one of our soldier boys, with an inch of candle
in hand, bestrode the trunk, as coolly as he would have
mounted a mule, and slid down into the under world.
His venture was rewarded, for far under the hill, upon
a shelf of rock, he found the bones of a man, and
beside him, within reach of the crumbling hand, an
extinguished torch.   The story was meagre but it was
all there: "there lived a man;" he set out to explore
that hollow artery of the mountain; he grew bewildered, wearied, and the light of his torch and the light
of his life went out pretty nearly together.   No matter
for his name; he died so long ago that nobody
remembers that he ever lived; they that mourned him
have been mourned in turn.   So, in caves and out of
them, "runs the world away."   The soldier generously
offered me a memorial bone,—say, of the forearm—as
he told the story.   I declined the bone but kept the
story.   But of course the boy managed to grave
his autograph at the entrance of the cave, for the
American man has a passion for scribbling.   He begins
by scrawling his name in every fly-leaf of his spelling-
book—" Jim Boggs—his book"—he goes on by writing
for the newspapers, and he ends by tracing that same
illustrious patronymic upon everything he can reach.

He has been known to peril his neck to inscribe it on the everlasting arch of the Natural Bridge of Virginia. He would have appended it to the old stone tables of the law, had he been in the corps of Moses.

But what has this to do with illustrating the desolation of war, asks some reader. I will tell him: visit any one of those clefts and caves, and a *cat* will be sure to put on her rough angry coat and growl at you; a cat will dart out of the cave as you go in, followed by another and more yet, until a perfect cataract of cats pours over the ledges and down into the evergreens. You can see them everywhere; cats grizzled and mottled, white and black and gray. It will amuse you till you begin to think of it, and then, when it occurs to you that these creatures were once tenants of hundreds of households; purred the winter nights out by hearths the armed stranger now treads upon; pets of children now scattered and gone; that if the people have not called upon the rocks of the mountains to hide them, at least the cats have fled to the caves, and are fast relapsing into a strange, fierce wildness, then you begin to understand the desolation of the land. Those houseless creatures tell you as plainly as if they spoke English with most miraculous organ, "there are no homes among these mountains!" And this is the hint of desolation. But to turn from the

caves of the mountains to human habitations, perhaps
no better idea can be gained of how rough the touch
of War is, even at the gentlest, than a look about
these headquarters. The grounds in front show traces
of the hand of taste, and that hand a woman's.
Graceful shapes, some day beautiful with flowers,
written over with the autograph of dead and gone
springs, are now trampled beneath the feet of orderlies;
and groups of horses, fastened to the trees, stamp upon
the broken borders of boxwood. The fences are swept
away; the summer-house has been torn down, trellis
by trellis, for kindling wood; tents fill the spaces
among the evergreens; sentries pace in paths where
ladies used to linger, and army wagons craunch through
the garden turned out to common.

Within, are suggestive souvenirs of the old time;
the curtains are removed, but the gilded supports
remain; a tall and ancient clock ticks away in the
corner, marking Federal time as faithfully as if its
master were not recreant. Very grand, in its day, was
that clock. Among the books left is an Album belonging to some "Ada," daughter of this house; its pages
filled with crow-quill assurances of love forever, by
girls, dating all the way from New Orleans to Chattanooga; its dainty little devices of hearts and doves
scrawled over with rude soldier comments in huge

soldier fists. But three living relics of the old regime
remain: "Aunt Jane" yet nods her turbaned head,
lone queen of the kitchen, and her button-headed boy,
Bill, kicks up his heels on the broken porch or swings
from the grape vine as he wills, "for massa's gone
away." Last but not least, the great honest New-
foundland, "Shiloh," watches the opening door for the
children that shall never come again, or runs distract-
edly about, called many ways, like Mercury, by many
masters. Thus the "darkeys" and the dog are the
sediment in the empty cup of chivalry.

You sometimes encounter so remarkable a fitness in
things as to suggest the doubt whether there is any
such thing as accident. Thus, the exact locality in
Chattanooga, whence I have written many letters, is a
two-winged mansion, a little inclined to be stately,
wherein aforetime the Gothic North got used to being
buttered and eaten like a sweet potato, and the shell
of the Union was regularly cracked with the walnuts
at aristocratic desert. A painting in oil covered the
wall above the mantel in the room where I passed
many an anxious day, crowned at last with a few
golden hours of exultation. I had been there days
and had only given it a careless look, for an army
forever on the eve of battle does not furnish the
surroundings most favorable for fine-art contemplation.

But one night as I sat in a lazy mood, my eyes rested upon the picture brought out by the flashes of the sweet, cedar fire.   It was Arnold and Andre conferring by the light of " a lantern dimly burning," on the banks of the Hudson.   The treason lay between them in certain folded papers ; the trick of the lantern lit up the features of traitor and martyr ; I was surprised to find it a startling and effective picture.   And there, in the gloomy background, the three patriots were waiting —Paulding, Williams and Van Wirt.   Find me, if you can, place and picture more accurately adjusted than this Arnoldic faith in this old homestead of secession.

Two Sundays ago, had you strolled beyond the picket line where Mission Ridge trends away to the South, you would have come upon an old homestead standing " where once a garden smiled," the ruined, fenceless grounds lying blank and bare.   The meaning of the word " desolation," not to be found in lexicons, is written along the face of all these regions.   Think of the dumb field that makes no answer to the blessed sun.   And the people only add human intensity to the picture, for they look like men and women whose almanac is a fragment ; *people without a to-morrow ;* and if there be anything in this world more desolate, I have yet to see it.   It was a lovely morning and the sun brought out the picture painfully ; the silent threshold, the orchard standing like broken ranks after a battle. You strike upon the door, and it returns a hollow sound like a clod upon a coffin-lid. And yet the birds, brave in the loneliness, sang all the same. A poor, old horse, was feebly grazing near by, and a man sat on the ground by the angle of the wall, reading. A few words told the story: that man was once the head of the vanished household; of that little firm there had once been more than enough to say "ours." A son whom he had educated, became principal of the Academy at Rome, was conscripted, and his fate unknown. Stripped of all, garner empty, fields unsown, the little band wandered away, and now he came, that pleasant morning, on a lonely pilgrimage, to linger out the day around what was the very ceno-taph, the empty burial place, of a dear, old home. Of how much tender and delicate sentiment those scattered and strown inmates were possessed, I cannot tell. Probably not much, and it was better so, for if GOD does not always "temper the wind to the shorn lamb," he sometimes blesses the creature with tough endurance.

A LATE BREAKFAST AT CHATTANOOGA

The January days of the year '64, when the first train of cars was vainly waited for, were long—winter days though they were—and the nights disastered. Clerks in the Departments held their pens poised in air, the word unfinished upon the page, as they listened for the shriek of the coming train. Soldiers intermitted duty as they bent a strained ear toward the angle of the wall of Lookout. Even hard bread was a luxury; they would have picked up the crumbs in thankfulness that fell from poor men's tables. Somebody—I think it was Liebig—said, that one man who eats beef and another who eats bread view a difficulty from entirely different stand-points; that a man's dinner "flies into his head" by the same sign that it goes into his stomach; that what he eats makes thought as well as muscle. And so, to learn a people thoroughly, you must either examine their larders, smell their chimney smokes, or stroll through their markets. I wonder how the Professor would locate the stand-point at Chattanooga.

The mules and horses were starving, and gnawed the rugged bark from the trunks of trees. That day was a

Tuesday; Wednesday went and no train. Men thought
they heard it a thousand times, but it was only the
sough of the wind among the mountains. Thursday
came, and men's faces grew fixed like daguerreotypes;
there was but one anxious expression on them all.
They lifted up their eyes and saw Bridgeport and Stevenson and Nashville filled with abundance and for
them, and here Famine looking them full in the face!
They were like men athirst in the desert, for whom the
magic of the mirage lifts the clear waters with their
cool margins of green, and mocks with the shadow of
blessing their dry and dying eyes. At last a faint and
distant cry, then nearer and clearer, till it whistled
down the winter wind.

Encampments swarmed and all men worshiped
toward the mountain. And then, with its plume of
smoke, the engine came creeping round on the wall of
Lookout, like a fly, and after it trailed three platform
cars laden with men and tools. Slowly it felt its way
over the rebel track, round the fearful curves, on to the
town; then to and fro, steaming up here, backing
down there, and, at last, wheeling upon its heel at the
turn-table, away went the engine with the only platforms ever heard of that all men could agree on,
round the fore-foot of the mountain and was out of
sight. Men took a long breath; homely as it all was,

it was an avant courier they had seen ; the pioneer of great joy. A few hours went by—but men could afford to wait then ; nobody was famished then—and seven trains, laden with the staff of life, came thundering through the valley, and poured their treasures into the empty lap of Chattanooga. And it is a Thursday they take for Thanksgiving.

A POTOMAC TRIP IN WAR TIME.

A drop down the Potomac in a splendid day is a thing to be remembered. The undulating shores, crowned with groves, spangled with gardens, dotted with mansions, tipped on the sky-line with forts, and finished out with flags, present an exquisite picture. Milder than the Hudson, grander than the Connecticut, and lovelier than either. We make out into the stream, and, looking back, have a view of the Chain Bridge, a canary-bird cage flung for a full mile across the broad river. At our right, looking out from among the trees, lifts the columned front of Arlington House, the abandoned home of General Lee ; at our left swells over the city the dome of the Capitol, that, like Lookout at Chattanooga, you can never lose sight of. Villas, encampments, golden checkers of grain fields,

spires and plumes of foliage, landings, and there, almost
in our front, the ancient city of Alexandria, clustered
in the valley, and sitting grandly about upon the hills.
Following the sweep of the Potomac, we make Fort
Foote upon the left, a bold, bluffy work, able to load
iron on hostile vessels a thought or two faster than
they can stow it away.

But the scene on the river will make you forget its
shores. There is everything in sight but a Venetian
gondola and a Chinese junk. Coming, going, at
anchor; with one wing a-flutter; with canvas piled in
pyramids, cloud above cloud; under bare poles;
steaming it to and fro. We meet fine, sea-weedish
ocean-going steamers, the slender tracery of their side-
wheels looking more like a spider's web than things to
walk the water with. These steamers are black-and-
blue as a pugilist's eye with soldiers; the yards dotted
with them; the figure-head bestridden by a bold
soldier boy. There goes a North River steamer, as
light and home-like as a country villa. A couple of
canal boats are drifting lazily down to Alexandria; a
sea-gull of a yacht is bracing up to the wind there;
saucy little tugs, with their noses out of water, and a
frill of a wake about their sterns like a scalloped petti-
coat, are screaming their way yonder. One of them
cuts in under our bows and scuds away before us as

impudently as a dog-fish. It is a curious truth that it takes a little creature to be impudent; your human tugs and terriers are as brassy as a "Napoleon gun." You pass a gunboat, homely as a mud-turtle; you are hailed by a guard-ship as black and sleek as an old-time snuff-box. Our blades dip dull wood and rise glittering silver; tubs of vessels seem oscillating in one place for an hour together, while arrowy craft dart around them like swallows on a mill-pond. Among the flock of various craft you will be sure to notice a dark, rakish-looking vessel, sharp in the nose, long in the body, with its two black chimneys at half-cock, and its masts a-tilt, and altogether making you think of Captain Kidd, "as he sailed." The craft are as varied as a sailor's notions, but they are all alike in one thing; from the cockle-shell of a sail-boat to the ocean-going monster, they all carry the flag; vast and broad, and flapping like an eagle's wings, or slight and fluttering as Desdemona's handkerchief, it is the flag still. This gorgeously inscribed fly-leaf of the Republic floats everywhere here.

IN MEMORIAM.—AD ASTRA.

There is one, away there in Georgia, of whom I think with an aching heart—Brigadier General Charles S. Harker. So young—not twenty-nine—so courteous, so generous, so modest, so winning, so gallant, "with an eye that takes the breath '—can it be the shot was ever moulded that could chill such vigorous life, and still a heart so noble! A Colonel, at first, of the 65th Ohio, he was at Shiloh, at Corinth, at Stone River, at Chicamauga, at Mission and Rocky Face Ridges, and a hero everywhere! I knew him well. With the frankness and simplicity of a boy he united the dash of a Marion and the wisdom of a veteran. I saw him earn his "stars," at Mission Ridge, as he led on his brigade like the tenth wave of the sea, right into the hell of splintery fire and shattered shell. I saw him the next morning, and nothing about himself—not a word—but everything about some valiant lieutenant, some gallant fellow in the rank and file. I had to go elsewhere for the details of his own story. And he is dead! For them that loved him longest, God strengthen them. Young General, good night;

Good night to thy form, but good morn to thy fame!

While threading a guerrillaish forest road with a
Division pushing on to the Front, we came to a deep
mountain run bridged with logs. "Here," cried one
of the boys, "is the old star-gazer's bridge," for so was
General O. M. Mitchell, commanding the First Division
of the Fourteenth Corps, known in the army. "Here,"
they said, "in a rainy night as dark as a wolf's mouth
he drew his woolen, plunged into mud and water,
tugged at the logs and worked like a beaver, and when
the bridge was done, off with his hat and cried, 'now
boys, three cheers for the minute bridge!' and they
were given with a will."

And yet that man was at first one of the most unpop-
ular of generals. The men, impatient of restraint,
worked restively in the snug harness of rigid discipline.
Some of them even muttered threats of making his
quietus with a bullet on some fighting day. He was
everywhere, at all hours, wherever men had duty to do;
he was severe, stern, and, as some thought, heartless.
But when duty, hardship and danger came in a cluster
within reach of his hand, and he plucked it with a
ready grasp and the lion's share, and the word was
"*come*, boys," and not "go," then the discipline he had
given them worked like a charm. Admiration followed
distrust, love succeeded hate, and when the brief his-

tory—alas, how brief!—ended, the proud record might well be graven on his monument:

His men would have died for him!

A Division General turned abruptly to me with, " If you write anything about Wednesday's affair, as you will, don't forget Colonel Miller, of the 36th Illinois— one of the most gallant little fellows that ever drew a sword." I did not need that injunction, for Colonel Silas Miller rode through the storm to the summit of the Ridge at the head of his regiment like a veteran, inspiring his men till the little 36th was a phalanx of heroes. The Colonel used to be adjutant of types and lead a column, now and then, in the old days, and, true to his early love, he headed a column at Mission Ridge. But before The March to the Sea was fairly begun, the noble soldier obeyed the Great Commander and lay front-face to the stars. The 36th, twelve hundred strong a breath or two ago, but now a skeleton regiment—and yet its soul of fire within those ribs of death!—bearing a banner whereon were blazoned such words as " Perryville ' and " Pea Ridge," went into the battle at Chattanooga with four hundred and fifty men, and stacked, when they came forth from the fiery baptism, one hundred and fifty-nine guns. Not a man in the broken ranks but will answer for him when Fame

calls the roll, as did his comrades for the dead grenadier
of old.   Not in our day shall Silas Miller want a tongue
to speak for him and answer " Here ! "

Eight years ago, a week after the battle of Chicamauga, the following paragraphs were written.   In the
light of history the world confirms the judgment :
When you read the story of the immortal " Hill
Difficulty," whereon General Thomas planted, on that
battle-Sunday, at Chicamauga, a grander growth than
ever crowned one little hill before, if you exalted
George Henry Thomas to a very lofty niche, you may
just leave him and History will keep him there forever.
I do not assert that he saved the Army of the Cumberland, but I believe he did ; that the salvation was not a
lucky blunder, but the result of brains as well as guns ;
that it was a disposition of force to defeat the enemy's
design, struck out with a rapidity so wonderful and a
wisdom so masterly that a month of mathematics would
not have materially modified the adjustment.   It was a
stroke of what, for the want of a better name, we must
call genius.   Not one of those men that draws his
sword every time he bids you good morning, General
Thomas is, perhaps, the most modest.   Combining the
energy, resolution and tenacity of the soldier with the
simple manners of a gentleman, he can handle a corps
and make a hammer or an anvil of it at will, and yet

he is one of the few in the Cumberland Mountains who does not believe he could handle the Cumberland Army. Meeker than his Second Lieutenants, he thinks quite as well of his peers as he does of General Thomas.

Do you know how he looks? Well, if you will just think what manner of man he must be that should be hewn out of a large square block of the best-tempered material that men are made of, not scrimped anywhere, and square everywhere—square face, square shoulders, square step; blue eyes, with depths in them, withdrawn beneath a pent-house of a brow, features with legible writing on them, and the whole giving the idea of massive solidity, of the right kind of a man to " tie to," you will have a little preparation for seeing him as he is.

Thus ran the record eight years ago, and now the war-cloud over and gone, Death found him where he sat in the midst of his friends, and no foe within all the broad horizon. You recall that dread, tempestuous day when

> 'Mid the gusts of wild fire, when the iron clad rain
> Did ripen brown earth to the reddest of stars,
> And baptized it anew and christened it Mars.
> In that moment supreme, to their bridles in blood,
> Like a rock in the wilderness grandly *he* stood
> Till the Red Sea was cleft and he rode down the street
> With the fame on his brow and the foe at his feet !

Oh, be muffled, ye drums!   Let artillery toll!
Cloud up, all ye flags!   Earth has lost a great soul.
Gallant THOMAS, good night, but good morn to thy glory,
Outranking them all in the charm of thy story!
Like a shadow in sunshine they have borne thee in state
Far across the new world to the true "Golden Gate"—
Philip Sidney, make room, for thy comrade is late!

KEEPING HOUSE UNDER DIFFICULTIES.

When people hear of an army's being on half-rations, they are apt to think of a man's eating his boots or his brother, or some such tough morsel.   So far from this, the soldier does not live who can eat his full ration and have life enough left to quote Shakespeare, "thou canst not say *I* did it!"   Eating a whole ration is eminently an irrational act.   Ordinarily it would make a man as torpid as an anaconda after swallowing a buffalo.   On the contrary, the men drive brisk bargains with their surplus rations, and very absurd stories could be told of the trades they strike up.   Half of them are locomotive groceries, and always on the *qui vive* for a barter.   To be sure, you will not see the delicate bones of many quails strowing the camps, or hear much of oysters on the half shell; the food is coarse but abundant.   I have sat down to a cup of coffee

that would make an Arab call upon Allah and the
Prophet, if he could get his breath, and have eaten
pork as rusty as the swords of the dead Knights
of Malta,

"Whose souls are with the saints, we trust;"

have attacked a cracker, and no man could declare that
I went hungry away.   Half rations does not mean
half starved.

I can tell you, though, when the Federal cause and
the Federal army were both in uniform and both decidedly blue, and the Federal larder was about as bare as
the cupboard of Mother Hubbard.   It was in the fall
of '62, when General Buell began to worship the North
Star, and Nashville was in a state of siege for three
such months as it only takes six of to make a round
year.   Inside, the city swarmed with enemies; there
was one of them at every soldier's elbow; they fronted
Headquarters, they flanked Headquarters, they wore
pantaloons, they wore petticoats, they toddled about in
rifle-dresses, they almost rustled in long-clothes.   Outside, there was a perfect *cordon* of foes; courier after
courier was sent out who never got through or never
returned; Nashville was hermetically sealed.

General Negley was in command, and Captain
Edwin F. Townsend of the 16th U. S. Infantry, in

charge of the Ordnance Department. But then it was nearly a department without any ordnance, though the enemy in the city did not suspect it. A train was laid to the magazine and it was solemnly announced that should the outside rascals attack the town and worse come to worst, why that train would be set off, and the inside rascals and Nashville would be blown out of the State of Tennessee. This pleasant assurance kept them all in a distracting state of hoping and fearing. Ten thousand tons of powder could not have done better execution so long as the Captain did not light the train !

Sunday after Sunday was set for Morgan and Breck-enridge's coming. How their friends within the city knew it, no man could divine, unless they discerned their approach in the tainted air. But they would gather in little knots in the streets, both men and women, and it was as plainly read as if their faces had been fresh-lettered guide-boards, whenever they had any welcome intelligence. Many a Saturday night, turkeys were killed and dainties prepared in expectation of their gray-clad knights of rescue, and in a mansion adjoining the quarters of Captain Townsend, the lady actually spread her bounteous table, on one of the hopeful Sabbaths, for the special delectation of John Morgan. The forces within the city stood thus: five

thousand Federal troops and two thousand Confeder-
ates ready to rise.   The General and his officers acted
with the utmost energy, but they were like Sterne's
starling—"they couldn't get out;" nay, worse than
that, they were like cats in a bag, they could not see
out; the enemy, his numbers and proximity were mysterious; the friend, his position and purpose were alike
unknown.

Perhaps nothing will give a more vivid idea of how
near they were to playing Robinson Crusoe, than a
little incident.   Two or three times during the siege,
adventurous persons in disguise, and by a circuitous
route—as if one hundred and eighty-five miles from
Louisville to Nashville were not miles a-plenty!—
worked their way through the lines with a Louisville
paper in their pockets, old enough, had it been a puppy,
to have had its eyes open five days!—and the Union,
the only paper in the besieged city, paid twenty-five
dollars for the copy, and straightway dispensed small
portions in extras, to a struggling crowd starving for
tidings from "the rest of mankind."   At night the
dwellings were locked up from the outside with
bayonets; there was no other way; it was a city of
enemies.

But those days, whose story has never been written,
were not idle ones.   Strong fortifications were thrown

up, and every preparation was made for a stout defense.
Not an ounce of cannon-powder in Nashville, the Ordnance officer set about emptying disabled cartridges, of
which he had as many as of effective ones, and pulver-
izing charcoal to incorporate with his cartridge glean-
ings, that the mixture might behave as cannon-powder
should, and burn with more dignified deliberation.
And then about the canister: they had no tin, but they
found and confiscated it ; and that done, the sides of
the canisters made, how about the ends?   They found,
in a coffin warehouse, sheet-iron cut to the pattern of
that last piece of furniture mortal man is supposed to
want, and it was just the thing.   They did not direct
that iron from its original purpose so very much ; instead of boxing up the dead foe, it was only to box up
death to him.   Thus they made six hundred rounds
and were ready for business.

Were they?   They had forts, but how about the
guns?   Well, they found down at the landing by the
Cumberland river, lying flat as a raft of logs, guns that
the enemy had stolen here and there—some from the
Norfolk Navy Yard—all stolen but one, and as to that,
they pilfered the materials of which they made it—a
columbiad marked " Memphis."   These guns were all
loaded, some with three charges of powder, and spiked
when the chivalry departed, but the garrison made

wheels and mounted them, and put them in position, and had nine twenty-four-pounders and four one-hundred-pound " Parrotts " as a part. of their armament, and were ready for business.

Were they? They had guns, but how about the shot and shell? And so they took to digging around the town, and prying into improbable places, and the hidden shot and shell turned out a bountiful crop. And the secession women were delighted at last. Morgan and Breckenridge appeared over the edge of the hills. Our guns showed their teeth and growled at them twice, and they slipped back out of sight to make ready for new approaches. To bring a brief story of long days to an end, one fine day—" December " *was* "as pleasant as May" that morning !—about eight o'clock, the cavalry vanguard of the army of Rosecrans clattered on to the bridge and streamed into the city; and so boxed up had the besieged been, that they did not know the army had left Bowling Green till its troopers rode through their narrow horizon into sight. And so ended the story of the Robinson Crusoes of Nashville.

"*NEARNESS OF MIND.*"

In war, if anywhere, men must sleep with the soul, like the revolver, under their pillows—must have what the old Greeks called nearness of mind, and their wits, like their weapons, within easy reach   So Farragut, the Admiral, lashed to the mast-head like Ulysses passing the Isle of the Syrens, when his ships went courtesying like stately dames into the Bay of Mobile, always kept his wits where he could find them in the dark; the man who, when the Southern lady asked him why he did not take Charleston, and was he not afraid of Fort Morgan, replied, " Madam, if I were ordered to take ' the *other* place ' I would *sail* for it ! " Nothing so inspires the rank and file with faith in their leaders— the faith that tones men up and makes more and nobler of them than there was before.   It is the principle recognized by the great Frederick when he addressed his General: " I send you against the enemy with sixty thousand men." " But, sire," said the officer, " there are only fifty thousand." " Ah, I counted *you* as ten thousand," was the monarch's wise and quick reply.   I have a splendid illustration of this in an incident that occurred on the dreadful Sunday at

Chicamauga. It was near four o'clock on that blazing afternoon, when a part of General James B. Steedman's division of the Reserve Corps bowed their heads to the hurtling storm of lead, as if it had been rain, and looked at each other, and betrayed signs of breaking. The line wavered like a great flag in a breath of wind. They were as splendid material as ever shouldered a musket, but then what could they do in such a blinding tempest? General Steedman rode up. A great, hearty man, broad-breasted, broad-shouldered, a face written all over with sturdy sense and stout courage, he realized the ideal of my boyhood, when I used to read of the stout old Morgan of the Revolution. Well, up rode Steedman, took the flag from the color-bearer, glanced along the wavering front, and with that voice of his that could talk against a small rattle of musketry cried out, "Go back, boys, go back, but the FLAG can't go with you!"—grasped the staff, wheeled his horse and rode down into the harvest of death. Need I tell you that the column closed up, grew firm and true and tempered as steel, swept down on the foe like a blade in the archangel's hand, and made a record that shall live when their graves are as empty as the cave of Machpelah! The blood of the Minute-men of Concord and Lexington was not all lost in the thirsty earth of the Revolution.

Within the same hour and on the same field occurred one of those incidents that make the stoutest heart stand still. Word was brought to General Gordon Granger of the Reserve Corps, in the midst of the tempest, that a certain regiment had but one round of ammunition. The blessed saltpetre was expected every moment, but it had not come. "But one round of ammunition, have you?" said the General. "Go back and tell them to fix bayonets, to *save* that one round—to lie down and wait till the enemy are within eight feet, to deliver their fire and give them the balance in cold steel. May I depend on you?" "You may," was the reply, and the trust was well placed, and the pledge was honored.

WAR AND WORDS.

No one has failed to observe the effect of the War upon common speech. It shuts the old-time tedious talks together as if they were telescopes the observers had done with. It makes people sharp, short and decisive as a telegram. When the men of the 79th Pennsylvania presented their colonel with an elegant sword, the speech and the reply were like two sweeps of a sabre: "Colonel, here is a bully sword—it comes

from bully fellows—take it and use it in a bully
manner!"

And the Colonel cut back again with, "Captain, I
accept the bully gift—that was a bully speech—let us
take a bully drink!" The whole ceremonial dwindled
down to something as direct as a duel and as brief as
a proverb.

One April evening, while in Lookout Valley, General
Hooker had a grand time clearing his guns of rust,
bringing his batteries into brisk play in the semblance
of a battle. Right, left and center, the columns of
white smoke rolled up over the valley's brim and hung
in heavy clouds over the scene. It was a regular set-to
of loud talk, but, like some speakers we have heard,
the words were round and fine, but the meanings had
somehow gone out of them. William the Quaker cannot conceive quite as well as William the Conqueror,
how much more eloquent and momentous are the utterances of artillery as heard in battle than when resonant
with the empty thunders of the blank cartridge.
Even the directest of soldiers do not object to speech,
but they want the fire delivered from shotted guns.

A little while ago you might have listened out half
a session, in Representative Hall or Senate Chamber,
and never heard one word that would prove the
prophetic day unborn, when the leopard and the lamb,

the lion and a little child shall make up the happy
family of "the good time coming." But now, you can
hardly be there an hour that the nation's new and
bloody business does not intrude; debate is broken in
upon by tidings from our armies in the field; the very
dialect of war has crept into legislative speech; the
Senator "changes his base" or "flanks" his opponent
or "carries the works." The Representative "steals
a march" or leads "a forlorn hope" or delivers an
"enfilading fire."

And this new tongue has gone into the sacred desk
as well. The "God of battles" is the being to whom
they pray, and the declaration of the Great Apostle
to the Gentiles, "I have fought the good fight—I have
kept the faith," is deemed as much the utterance and
the epitaph of the true soldier as of him who stood on
Mars' Hill, for do not we all stand on Mars' Hill? It
is "the sword of the Lord and of Gideon," and "the
soldier of the Cross," and "terrible as an army with
banners" they tell us of; the war-horse of Job is as
bright as a new picture, and the story of those out-
stretched arms, sustained till the going down of the
sun, while the battle rolled on, is read with an interest
before unknown. Illustrations are no longer plucked
from the gentle Sermon on the Mount; the lilies of
the field and Sharon's roses bloom on untouched.

Even a piece of artillery is christened out of the beatitudes—those melodious blessings that hang like a chime of bells in the very top of the Saviour's speech, and "blessed are the peacemakers" is translated out of the original Greek into the dialect of gunpowder.

ALEXANDRIA IN '64.—SOLDIERS' REST.

A steam ferry, asthmatic and greasy, is a very slender provocation to much poetry, but when the boatman threw out the line, and I set foot on shore, I could not forget it was my first touch of "the mother of Presidents." A narrow street, paved with boulders, invites you grimly, and a barricade thrown across it lets you through its ponderous gateway. You go banging up the street as if you were riding a trip-hammer. The signs that glare at you along the river are suggestive—"Plaster mills and Guano"—and you remember that the "sacred soil" is worn so poor and thin that it needs all sorts of tonics to keep it up, for the sweat of the brow that used to fall there never yet fattened the ground it fell on. But the fields of "the old Dominion" are growing richer, day by day, and the rain is red that waters them. GOD clear away the cloud.

In Alexandria five Colonial Governors met, almost an
hundred years ago, and hence Braddock set forth on
the expedition from which he never returned. The
church yet stands that claims a dead vestryman in the
man of Mount Vernon. Like a quiet, old Virginia
gentleman, with nothing to do, Alexandria sits by the
Potomac, seven miles below Washington, and lazily
watches the dome of the capitol all the long summer
afternoons. But its sleepy glory has departed, and it
has pulsated like a great heart, and through it men
have throbbed out to battle by the hundred thousand,
and rations by millions.

Going through the old burial places of the ancient
city, you reach a beautiful spot of seven acres, only a
little breadth of the ridged and mighty field of graves.
It is the United States Military Cemetery in Virginia.
Begun in 1862, the willing years have helped the taste-
ful hands; tree, flower and shrub lend fragrance and
beauty; a monument is to lift its graceful shape, a sort
of strange vignette with a broad border in Death's
hand-writing all around. At the right, as you enter,
the white head-boards glitter in the sun. Two thousand three hundred and forty-six of them already—a
whole brigade of soldiers fast asleep! Here and there,
a tablet bears that dreary word, "Unknown;" many
show the touch of a loving hand; all are laid like

Christians in their beds of peace. A little building in the center, flanked with a green-house, is occupied by a clerk in charge, who dwells in the heart of that strange, silent neighborhood. It is proposed to erect a monument in the center of this acre of GOD, and contributions are daily made. Many a boy in blue passes along the breathless ranks, and, turning away, leaves his little offering for his dead comrades' sake, thinking, I dare to say, not once in a thousand times that perhaps he is paying a tribute for his own.

Approaching the Cemetery, I fell into line behind a funeral procession, and so passed within the white gate of the field of silence. There were three ambulances, each bearing a stained coffin covered with the flag. Twelve soldiers marched with them to this edge of the living world, and there drew up in line, with uncovered heads, beside the open graves. As the coffins one after one were lowered, the drums gave three low ruffles, as sad as a sighing, and the sword of the officer sank reverently earthward. And then, the Chaplain stood forth and read, "Lord, hadst thou been here my brother had not died;" and then he prayed a soldier's prayer, for the flag and them that bear it; the ambulances wheeled away, the escort filed after them, the fifes and drums struck up a merry tune—"so dies in human hearts the thought of death "—and the strange pageant, bare and severe as if a Puritan had planned it, was ended.

And yet it was such a scene as would leave a lithograph on the heart. Rachel was not there; no veiled and speechless sorrow. I thought of the mother, sister, sweetheart, wife, and, for the moment, I stood mourner in her stead. I looked around as the simple rites went on. Negroes, that were digging graves and making paths had ceased their work, and stood with uncovered heads all over the cemetery; one grizzled sexton, the "Uncle Tom" aforetime of some old plantation, knelt, his gray head bowed between his hands, four or five little atoms of Africa that had been dropping pebbles in a waiting grave—the man not dead who yet should be its tenant!—stood dumb and dark as the head of a note in a musical score, each with his box of ivory shut tight; and they all made a striking picture of the proverbial reverence of the race. But a robin on a tree near by sang as if nothing had happened, and the sun shone on, as if there were no clouds in the world save those that float in heaven.

WASHINGTON IN JULY, '64.

Washington, "the only child of the Union," has tendencies to ague. Perhaps it is not strange, since in 1814, it had a chill and a flash of British fever that should have crimsoned England with the blush of shame. From the beginning of this war it has had repeated attacks of the old complaint, and shivered in its shoes with the fear of the enemy.

Surely, never was child so girded with an iron zone. A sweep of forty miles of massive works, encircling both Alexandria. and the capital, studded with almost sixty forts, filled in with sixty batteries more, ribbed with rifle pits, beaded with bombs, this battle sash of wonderful fabric woven in the loom of war, is bound about the Federal city.

It is Sunday morning, the tenth of July. That the enemy is within sixteen miles of Baltimore, and, like John Brown's soul, still "marching on," does not disturb this city's lazy lassitude; it just rises on its elbow and listens in the sun. To be sure, it hums a little around the hotels, but the more important movements go noiselessly on. The newsboys, as I finished that sentence, were rushing frantically by, crying "wolf" and the "extra" with voices like young roosters.

Bands of music, bodies of infantry and little clouds of cavalry begin to pass across the city; hard riders dash through the streets; engines are harnessed to the trains; steamers draw heavy breaths and give symptoms of waking; the treble of the newsboys flaunting their second extra, and singing out, "rebels a marchin' on to Washin'ton!" again startles you, and at last the city brushes the poppy leaves off its eyelids and is broad awake. It leans out of windows; it comes fairly out of doors; it ties itself in knots on street corners; it buys "extras" and reads them; it hears rumors and believes them; it whistles a little and tries to look unconcerned.

The President visits the works; heavy artillery and reserve guards are moved to the northern fortifications, and the capital is thoroughly aroused. But it need not be ashamed of a good honest sensation. Roast pig— according to Lamb, strangely enough—was a discovery. Washington has a sensation. Possibly it is not pleasant, but then it is a tonic. I stroll along the Avenue. Everybody from king to kaiser is saying "trenches— cavalry — defenses — rebels." Night comes, and the tramp of marching regiments beats the pavements, and the glittering barrels of muskets flash in the uncertain glimmer from windows along the way. It is the advance of the Sixth Corps, General Wright commanding, *en route* for Fort Stevens, and not a minute too soon. Probably no man in Washington—the. President not excepted—bore about with him so great a burden of care and solicitude as William H. Seward, the Secretary of State. From his point of observation the mere material destruction was immaterial ; it was not a question of battle lost or won ; of works carried or defended, but something above and beyond them all. The Atlases, with starry worlds on their shoulders, are dealing with sections of our own country, but his relations are with the civilized globe ; the feelings of an American North, in view of possible disaster, concern him less than the judgment of a watching World. It was this thought that may have lent a dignity to the raid it had not otherwise attained. With masterly skill he had kept the ship upon an even keel ; no nation on the planet had sought to bring it to, with a saucy gun ; what logic the Christendom across the sea would find in the mere suspicion that the Capital could be insulted, if not imperiled, might well provoke a thought. Whatever the Secretary might have felt, there was an unwonted briskness in his step ; he leaped into his carriage like a boy ; he rode out to the fortifications and watched the movements with an earnest eye. I do not think there was a trace of anxiety apparent ; but I believe that he was looking beyond

the battle-zone of Washington, beyond possible assault
and gallant defense, at the consequences of this strange
antic that might lie in the far future.

Monday the eleventh, the guns of the enemy can be
heard in the suburbs of the Federal capital; he threw
out his skirmish line at Tennally-town, and has slowly
advanced cityward; he appears near Silver Springs and
occupies the mansion of Montgomery Blair. The
farmers have turned their backs upon rural delights
and fled from green fields to gray pavements. Generals
Breckenridge and Early stood beneath the trees on Mr.
Blair's beautiful grounds, and saw the sunset upon the
dome of the capitol. Just beyond the Ridge lay fifteen
thousand of the enemy, and parks of artillery. All
those houses, the fringes of bushes and every conceivable shelter, swarmed with sharp-shooters, who picked
off our men upon the parapets, and to whom nobody
seemed out of range. Creeping up almost under the
muzzles of the guns, the whistle of the bullets would
admonish the cannoneer that little messengers fly on
grave errands. To the left of Fort Stevens, in the
Carberry House, the rebel sharpshooters had taken
shelter in most uncomfortable neighborhood, when a
shell from the Fort struck the cupola, and fairly
drummed them out of quarters.

So passed the day, and the enemy never showed his hand. His artillery was over the ridgy edge of the horizon, and never gave General Alexander McCook, in command of the northern defenses, a glimpse of it. His infantry, whatever he had, was there too; his fashion was to come down the hill with a heavy skirmish line, to feel us here and there, to scatter out into groves and bushes, and play squirrel hunter; then a crack or two from a heavy Federal whip, and away he went. He evidently thought the works were manned by clerks never under fire, and what he calls "condemned Yankees." He fairly snapped his fingers at us and played "the siege of Washington" Among the novelties he sent us were piano tuning-screws in place of bullets, and bits of chains and buttons, and all in all, he behaved in a very eccentric manner. Altogether, these fellows were a queer, mischievous, rollicking set. They brought along hymn books and song books; they wrote bad verses and pasted them upon trees; they left saucy letters for the President. They even brought along with them spelling books! General McCook showed me one belonging to James Regan, "his book," 29th Georgia regiment, and the first page I opened to read "The Fate of the Robber."

Tuesday morning finds the Federal capital humming like a bee in a hollyhock. Long guns sprouted with bayonets are going about in company with short clerks; black-coated civilians take the beat of blue-coated guards. Admiral Goldsborough has put a heavy force of his men in Fort Lincoln and the rifle-pits; General Rucker, Chief Quartermaster, has rallied an army from his Department, two thousand strong, and led them himself, as you might know he would, to look at him, out to Forts Stevens and Reno; the clerks in the Departments have "grounded" pens and shouldered arms and are drilling under the trees near the War Department, and everybody is tugging home some sort of a death-dealing tool. The Sixth Corps is in position; other troops are arriving; the enemy's opportunity, if he ever had one, is utterly gone, for "blue Monday" and the opportunity departed together.

Taking either Seventh or Fourteenth street, you leave the city, cross the old stamping ground of McClellan, pass beautiful residences, gardens and groves, and so, up hill and down dale, until you reach a "Uriah Heep" of a tavern, squatted by the roadside—the headquarters of General McCook. Just beyond stands Fort Stevens, a little ragged to look at, with an abattis of dry branches of trees under its chin, like a scraggy whisker, but a strong piece of War's

solid geometry for all that. You are three miles from
the border of Washington, looking north; Fort De
Russcy is to your left; Slocum to your right, and a
little nearer the city; Totten yet further to the east;
Lincoln more distant still, and beyond it to the northeast is Bladensburg. This fan-like section of the
northern defenses fronted the hostile apparition. A
heavily undulating sweep of landscape is before you.
Descending away from the Fort, you have a little,
shallow valley, three-fourths of a mile broad, then a roll
of the land, with a depression beyond, and then a
swelling ridge, perhaps a mile and a half distant, that
bounds the horizon. It is confused with shrubbery,
sprinkled with trees, dotted with homes.

And all the time. up to Tuesday evening—July 12th—
there had been no battle; only skirmishing and dashes
of cavalry and soundings of our line. Ransom's troopers, and squads of Imboden's command, and Mosby's
men, had broken out in spots all over the country
round about, like a case of malignant rash, but nothing
tangible; they melted out of hand like a wisp of
smoke. Meanwhile, our men were ready. Admiral
Goldsborough's blue jackets fairly made a frolic of it,
taking a hitch in their pantaloons and smoking their
pipes and keeping a jolly eye out for squalls, with as
much composure as if they were in the forecastle,
listening to Tom Longbow's last yarn.

The sun had burned its way clean through the day down into Tuesday afternoon, and the enemy in that orchard, you see yonder, was getting saucy. And then there would be a lull; and then, it was crack, bang and scatter; the gray and blue skirmish lines, within short pistol shot in places, and elsewhere widening away to rifle range, were playing "balance to partners." It looked very little like a battle; very much like the prefatory sparring of a couple of pugilists finding out the length and muscle of each other s arms.

The Sixth Corps were held well in hand, for they chafed a little at hanging round the heavy artillery, and were eager to strike out. The enemy's style of rushing up, delivering his fire, dodging behind trees and scudding back to cover, making a rabbit-warren of the landscape, was not at all to their liking. Things could not go on after this fashion. Under the darkness of the night, the enemy might advance his line, throw up breastworks within four hundred yards of the guns and pick off the gunners at his leisure. And so it was determined to find out what this Udolpho with his Mysteries was made of.

The charge was ordered at six o'clock, Tuesday evening, three guns the signal for moving out. At the last tick of the battle clock they went. The enemy, six full brigades, drawn up in two lines, watched and waited, and made no sign. They thought them clerks and invalids; handfuls of tow to be licked up at the first touch of fire. They hurled opprobrious epithets at them as they came, as if so they would save their gunpowder. Out into the open ground moved six sifted regiments—ah, with what terrible winnowing on old fields!—numbering eleven hundred men, led by Colonel Bidwell of the 49th New York; eleven hundred and no more. Fort Stevens let drive a salvo of artillery over their heads as they went. The enemy delivered his fire, but the Federal line, not scorched and curled like a leaf, came easily and steadily on. The enemy recognized them in an instant. Toughened to battle as a sailor is to the sea, the veterans of the Potomac pushed out into the open ground, and to use their own camp phrase, "sailed in." There was no mistaking them. "Are you there, Yanks?" was the cry, and then, "the Sixth Corps! the Sixth Corps is here, by G—d!" was shouted from rank to rank, and the rebels stiffened sinews stoutly, but it was useless. The old smoky fellows, that snuff the battle like the war-horse of Job, broke through the first line, and shut it back upon the second like the battered lid of an old book, and away went the six brigades into the hollow and over the hill, one and a half miles, by the memory of John Gilpin! It took sixty minutes in all, and that was the end of it and that was all of it. No, not all; for the defense of the city cost us three hundred and fifty in killed and wounded, and, as I write, they are engaged in the sad work of removing the dead who were buried upon the field, to a more befitting resting place. All who fell before the city are to lie as they fought, shoulder to shoulder, in one place.

In the morning, the whole "Front," for miles out, was as empty as a drum. They came here hungry and active, every man's belt drawn up to the last hole; empty stomachs make light heels. Their flocks and herds were well under way, every nose of them all pointed toward the Antarctic; their wagons, laden with "leather and prunella," and entertainment for man and beast, were stringing across the flat Potomac, the Sixth Corps was behind them, "there was no use knocking at the door any more."

THE SCOUT AND THE SPY.

There is a description of invaluable service requiring the coolest courage, and the clearest head and the quickest wit of any soldierly duty, but which, from its nature, seldom appears in print. I refer to the achievements of the scout. He passes the enemy's lines, sits at his camp-fire, penetrates even into the presence of the commanding General; he seems a Tennesseean, a Georgian, an Irishman, a German—anything indeed but what he really is; if he falls, no friendly heart may ever know where; his grave is nameless. The scout voluntarily signs away his right to be treated as a prisoner of war. If he is detailed from the ranks to render this special service, he is denounced as a deserter by his comrades and as a spy by the enemy. He takes his life in one hand and seeming dishonor in the other. Like the Nomades he reckons time by nights and not by days; he lurks like a wild creature in darkness when it is in his heart all the while to stand forth like a man in the day. "John Morford," known in civil life as Lewis Carter, and one of the most daring of Federal scouts, was found dead in the mountains near Chattanooga, and John Carlock, who had achieved fame for his tact and daring in the Department of the Cumberland, was killed by a com-rade, a member of the Anderson cavalry, whom he halted. The latter, supposing him to be an enemy, instantly fired a fatal shot. The story of Harvey Birch, as inimitably wrought up in Cooper's "Spy," lends at once a romance and a dignity to the office that has undoubtedly led many a brave fellow to peril life or to live it on under a cloud, in playing the role of the scout.

There is William Crutchfield. An old resident, and for years proprietor of the "Crutchfield House," knowing every road, stream, wood, hill, in all the country round, he has rendered invaluable service to the Federal cause; brigades have moved by routes he designated, and halted at camping grounds of his selection. A rough, angular, uncourtly man, of good, strong sense, I have heard him address Major-Generals as "you fellows," and rattle on about the geography of the region with more accuracy than a gazetteer. While he himself has been obliged to do considerable of what Leatherstocking would call "sarcumvention" to keep out of the enemy's hands, his family has remained at Chattanooga through all weathers. In one or two instances it rained iron on the old homestead, but the inmates lived on content, having read, perhaps, Marryatt's story of the Fire-eater, who escaped in battle, because he always put his head into the hole the first cannon ball made in the ship's side, as, according to Professor Truman, the odds were 32,647 and some decimals that another shot would never come in at the same hole.

Women—not invariably any " better than they should be "—have always been employed to persuade information out of suspected persons, and they bring a degree of tact and shrewdness into play that hirsute

humanity can never hope to equal. Many a wasp has
been caught with their honey of hypocrisy. A subor-
dinate Federal officer in Nashville had been long
suspected of disloyalty, but no proof to warrant his
arrest could be obtained, and so as a last resort a
woman was set at him. She smiled her way into his
confidence, and became his "next best friend," but,
finding that ears were of no use, for he could not be
induced to say one word of matters pertaining to his
office, she changed her plan of attack, and turned a
couple of curious and beautiful eyes upon him.

Frequently he would ride out of town into the country, be absent three or four hours and return. For all
the hours of the twenty-four but just these she could
account. Within them, then, lay the mischief if mischief there was, and she began to watch if he made
any preparations for these excursions. He loaded his
old-fashioned pistol, drew on his gloves, lighted a cigar,
bade her good by—"only that and nothing more."
Was he deep and she dull? Time would show. At
last, she observed that he put an unusual charge into
the pistol, one day, and all at once she grew curious in
pistols. Would he show her some day how to charge a
pistol, how to fire a pistol, how to be a dead shot?
And just at that minute she was athirst, and would he
bring her a lemonade? She was left toying with the

weapon, and he went.   The instant the door was closed
behind him, she drew the charge, for she knew quite as
much of pistols as he, and substituted another.   She
was not a minute too soon, for back he came, took the
weapon and rode away.   No sooner had he gone than
she set about an examination of the charge, and it
proved to be plans and details of Federal forces and
movements, snugly rolled together.   The mischief *was*
in the pistol, then, though none but a woman would
have thought of it, and so it was that he carried information to his rebel friends with rural proclivities.   The
woman's purpose was gained, and when the officer
returned, had vanished like an Arab or a vision, and he
had hardly time to turn about before he was under
arrest.

Admiring the adroitness of the achievement, we
cannot help regretting that a woman performed it.
The memory of a man's mother is sacred, and he feels
that whoever wears her form unworthily and debases
woman's graceful gifts, profanes it.

A DIVIDED HOUSEHOLD.

The complications caused by this most cruel war astonish me. I learned much of them in Georgia. Tennessee and Alabama, but they are even more sad in Washington. Young men disappeared from their homes on the Sunday of the enemy's approach, and the next I knew of them they were deploying into the hostile skirmish line. A few squares distant, one of those poor, misguided fellows is lying in his father's house, fearfully wounded, and by a Federal shot in front of Fort Stevens. So sure were the sympathizers of the capture of the capital that rooms long darkened were opened, swept and garnished, and preparations made to give high banquet to the conquering heroes.

In the Federal trenches before the capital was General Rucker, Chief of the Quartermaster's Department, and across the little valley was General Ransom, Chief of rebel cavalry, his old regimental comrade, as were Ewell and Longstreet. Rucker had a letter from the latter just as the little cloud of trouble, "no bigger than a man's hand," began to show in the horizon. Longstreet was with his regiment away on the frontier, and the boding sounds in the hollow air had reached him.

"What," he writes, "does it all mean? Is anything serious impending?" To General Rucker's reply that he trusted not, Longstreet substantially responded, "I hope to GOD you are right; that the dissolution of the Union is not threatened." This was his last loyal word to his old companion in arms, and the first audible monosyllable at Sumter found them arrayed face to face, enemies in war, though in peace they had been friends.

Take it at Chattanooga: Colonel Fullerton, Granger's Chief-of-Staff, and a Confederate officer are talking of old days beneath the white flutter of a flag of truce. They were once neighbors and friends. They belonged to a young men's club; there were thirty of them. Among them were Frost, Major-General in rebeldom, and Basil Duke. Twenty-six of them cast off their allegiance, as if it had been a worthless garment instead of a costly vesture that should have clothed their souls with honor; Colonel Fullerton and the three other true-hearted comrades stood by the old flag. Even the writer had two schoolmates over yonder on Mission Ridge; one of them a Colonel from the Palmetto State, the other risen to the doubtful dignity of a rebel General. Alas, for the days that are no more!

Look at the grand old Second Regular Cavalry, and you will marvel to see the rebel Generals file out of it; Robert E. Lee was its Lieutenant-Colonel; Albert Sydney Johnson, killed at Shiloh, belonged to it, and so did Generals Van Dorn, Hardee, E. Kirby Smith and Fitz Hugh Lee. So runs the tarnished, tattered roll of the dashing troopers of the old Second.

"Blood is thicker than water." At Murfreesboro two brothers lived apart and estranged for years only to meet face to face on that tremendous field, and more than one musket was turned aside in the flash of mutual recognition, that a brother's blood should not cry out from the ground.

Keep on entangling the world in the web of the telegraph; bind it a little more firmly with railroad bars; quicken, by a few plunges a minute, the shaft of the steam engine; affiliate men a little more in affairs sacred and secular by the agency of art, science, literature and religion, and foreign war in any accepted meaning of the term will be a thing impossible; the battle roll will be a record of sharper, bitterer struggles than have yet distracted the race, all kindled to the intensity of civil conflict. There will be neither Greek nor Barbarian, and from being the clash of organized mobs of strangers war will become the fiercer, deadlier strife of an alienated brotherhood.

THE WAR DEPARTMENT.

The thought saddens, as it goes the heavy rounds of the twenty-one hospitals in the Federal city, these July days of '64, where thousands languish, the stricken heroes from the battles of Virginia.   The leaves of the linden beneath my window, that swing at a breath, as if the tree were laden with the green pendulums of little French clocks all going at once, have "run down;" and there, a soldier's emblem of these broad, brazen days, they lie motionless upon the air.   With the poor, wounded boys, time, indeed, stands still.   I wish I could tell you, in words befitting, of the patience of those men;   how they treasure their terrible wounds;   no "Old Guard" of the Corsican so prized his cross of the Legion of Honor.   But they crave the gentle touch and voice of woman.   The "well done, my men!" of the commanding General is much, but the cup of cold water from a loving hand is more.   She is not represented in the Cabinet;   she has no voice in the Capitol, but in the thought and heart of the Federal armies she abideth forever.

Next to the hospitals, perhaps, the stranger regards the War Department with the deepest interest.   He

thinks of it, as the spot whence the slender nerves radiate, that move the mailed and clenched hand of the
Government, and hurl a million of men, like mighty
hammers, upon its enemies.   And so, he strolls up the
Avenue, by the great, white city and stately columns
of the Treasury ; by the sober front of the State Department ; by the uncertain magnificence of the President's
mansion ; and pauses at last before a brown brick building, three stories in height, with a little growth of white
columns at the entrance, and altogether, looking as
meek and harmless as a Ladies' Seminary.   No trace
of "the pomp and circumstance" anywhere.

It is Mars' horrid front hidden in a Quaker bonnet.
A foreground of green grass, dappled with the shadows
of linden, maple, ash and elm, completes the illusion,
and he expects to see a group of white-skirted girls
blossom out of the open door in the portico, any moment.   True, the iron fence, with its fasces tipped out
with tomahawks, and the escutcheon of cannon over
the entrance, and the gilded eagle, are a little suspicious ; and when he discerns a couple of soldiers' knapsacks lying beside the door, and sees "leaves" silver
and golden drifting on blue shoulders over the threshold, and now and then a "star ;" and hears the positive,
energetic step of the Secretary of War upon the pavement, and catches a glimpse of his next neighbor, the

President, coming across the shady green, the suspicion turns to certainty; the War Department is before him. There are the nerves I wrote of, strung away on to Sherman before Atlanta, and down to Grant before Petersburg, and out to banditti-haunted Missouri, and messages from fifty fields flock like doves to their windows; and it seems to him fitting they should come in flashes of lightning, and not, as of old, beneath the wing of "the bird let loose in Eastern skies," the carrier-pigeon. What tales of triumph and disaster, of wounds and death, have reached those chambers, as if the birds of the air had brought them. Perhaps he says to himself, "ah, no love messages there," but he thinks wrong. The grandest of love tokens have flickered in at that window: how men have given right hands and right hearts for love of liberty and land; how they are "married unto death" every day; how they press their bloody brows upon the breast of the bride, fall asleep under the flag and are content. There is no pageantry about that quiet building, and yet, there is no marble pile in Washington on which the thoughtful eye will linger with more earnest look.

Beneath the shade along the iron fence, a detachment of tired soldiers lies fast asleep on Jacob's pillow, the stony pavement. And may be, it is a Bethel to

some of them, too; and wife and child, or the girls they
left behind them, may be ascending and descending, in
the guise of angels, the silver ladder of a dream.

Leaving the gate of the Capitol to-night, I met an
old man hastening to the Baltimore cars. He carried
a sword tenderly upon his arm, as if it had been an
infant. And yet he was no soldier, and the weapon
was no new toy. He was a father, fresh from the June
fields of the West—the scabbard was battered and the
hilt was stained. He had given a son to GOD and
liberty, and was going home with the sword! It was
not the first time I had seen old swords borne northward by hands unused to wield them, but it was the
first time its full meaning had come home to me.

All this summer of the year of grace '64, Washington is thronged with strangers seeking a sorrow, or
a joy so like a grief that the tear will express it far
oftener than the smile. They come from New England
valleys and GOD'S Western pastures; from every State
that has a soldier in the Front. You will see men in
the home-made suit, and women in the garments of
some dead and gone fashion. Altogether, it is a
strange mingling of this new element of homeliness
and heart with the gay whirl of Vanity Fair. Five
hundred, a thousand miles these wanderers come, and

they all have one errand: they seek a soldier languishing. a brother wounded, a husband dying, a first-born
dead.

There are scenes almost every day that stand at the
door of the heart and knock audibly for entrance.
Take one incident from hundreds. I was fellow-
passenger with a lady bound for Washington, and she
was going upon the one errand. She had a son, a
young Lieutenant of Company E, 2d Michigan, who
was wounded the other day. Ah, how brave George
was, and how dutiful he was, and how—but it is all
told in this: he had a mother to love him. And she
was hastening to take care of the brave soldier; she
that his young eyes had worshiped, looking up as he lay
smiling in her arms, just twenty years ago.

"How long will you remain in Washington?" was
the question. "Till he is ready to go home," was the
quick reply. So, through the mountains of Pennsylvania, through the monumental city, sped the train.
The capital was reached; the location of the boy's
hospital ascertained, and the mother hurried away.
The next day I went to the hospital, but the mother
was not there. "Is Lieutenant George S. Williams, of
Company E, 2d Michigan, here?" The leaves of the
record are slowly turned, and the finger moves down

the lines, of name after name, in that roll of honor.
The finger halts at last: the officer reads,

"George S. Williams, Lieutenant, 2d Michigan,"

turns with a quick look and says, "died day before
yesterday!" "I shall stay till he is ready to go," were
the words of the mother, and he was ready, even while
she uttered them. Why not write upon his head-stone
for eulogy and epitaph,

"HE WAS READY TO GO!"

Ah, the bravery, in these battle years, is not all at
the Front! Bullets fly far, borne on from flight to
flight, northward, even as the silver arrow of Arabian
story, that, driven from the bow, led the archer a weary
way to a distant land.

TWO BATTLE FIELDS A YEAR OLD.

The arts of peace follow the battle, even as the
peaceful rainbow the grim and roaring cloud, and grain
grew rank at Waterloo, and violets fulled like the moon
and turned to pansies on the field of Inkermann. So
at Mission Ridge and Stone River.

The calm-faced clock that, across the Hall of Repre-
sentatives, forever looks the Speaker in the eye, has

seen laws born without emotion, and generations of legislators come and go, like shadows on a dial, without regret. With what patience it has timed dull speeches unnumbered; with what indifference it has told off little moments of eloquence; and how unrelentingly it lifts those bloodless hands to heaven in sign of twelve o'clock.

Were battle-fields as changeless as that clock's dead face; had the passing year no way of hiding the unseemly scars; did not the sharp acanthus sometimes turn Corinthian and crown a capital; did not time grow loving and smoothe the ridged and rolling graves till they subside at the caress, and, like the troubled sea at CHRIST'S command, have rest, how hideous a scrawl of War's wild autographs would mar the planet's disc!

It took ten tons of ammunition to fight the battle of Stone River, and here is Murfreesboro as calm as if it had always lain in the lap of peace. Asleep in the April sun of '64 lies the broken field of Stone River. Could I help regarding it with an earnest eye? The little thread of water in midsummer, but a torrent in spring-time, working its winding way between high banks to the North, curves abruptly toward the western side of Murfreesboro, and makes a horse-shoe where the enemy formed their line of battle, sixty-two thousand strong. You remember the closing words of Rosecrans in front of Murfreesboro on that New Year's eve:

"Be cool. I need not ask you to be brave. With GOD'S grace and your help, I feel confident of striking this day a crushing blow for the country. Do not throw away your fire. Fire slowly, deliberately—above all, fire low, and be always sure of your aim. Close steadily in upon the enemy, and when you get within charging distance, rush upon him with the bayonet. Do this, and victory will certainly be yours."

Asleep around me lie two thousand Federal dead. It is a broad Golgotha, a place of skulls. Were it not demonstrated that it takes about a man's weight of lead to kill him, I could never believe that from the hot places of the field, where the trunks of trees are honeycombed with bullets, and where your brothers and mine stood up to the storm without flinching, and sank beneath it without sorrowing, one man could have come forth alive. So hasty and imperfect was the sepulture, that yesterday, hands shriveled and blackened in the sun, looking like those of some mummy from the pyramid of Cheops, were visible, thrust out of the earth in mute appeal; and as a strange memento of the battle, the skeletons of a horse and his gray-coated rider were found, only the other day, lying where they fell, the missile passing through the thighs of the trooper and the body of the horse, and there

they lay together, the rider, the ridden, and the solid
shot. Our dead boys were decently buried, and head-
boards bearing the names and regiments of the sleepers
made check-work of the field; but already many of
these are gone, and of them who sleep under the little
ridges all traces are effaced forever.

The Federal fortifications cover three hundred acres,
and require a garrison of fifteen thousand men. Rifle-
pits, angles and willow bastions make a grand geomet-
rical diagram of the whole landscape, breaking it up
most strangely, to a man who had seen nothing more
formidable than an Osage-orange hedge planted to stay
the progress of errant flock and herd.

How wildly upon this spot the old year '62 closed in;
how red and angry was the glare that lighted on the
new! Standing here to-day I keep forgetting that I
look upon the scene of deeds that shall outlast the
house of the grave-maker. Amid the homely sounds
of common life, with only the snarl of an idle drum in
the distance, I cannot clearly trace the lines of fire
drawn here and yonder in the terrible geometry of
battle. In this lazy air I can hardly think how right
over my head the curtains of the thunder shook to the
top of heaven. The ranks of corn may wave along
these acres, and the monumental shaft sink wearily
away into the *Italic* of time, but these sleepers here

shall spring to resurrection in song and story, and Stone River be stereotyped among the battle-fields of Liberty.

How swiftly the plowshare follows the sword, no man can quite appreciate who has not seen from a single stand-point, the sweep of the one and the sober going of the other. Think of it! Where, last November, I saw Hooker move up to the battle in the clouds, his stout and steady legions swinging round the mountain disc, six plows are scarring a spot, the colters cutting the willing earth, these April days, for a potato-field! Horses that thundered bravely on in a charge of cavalry, are going soberly to and fro along the glistening furrows. Where, last November the crest of Lookout all day long gave growls of thunder, now stands the cabin of a photographer, and hundreds of groups has he taken at long range, standing upon its brink. Thus closely does trade tread upon the heels of war.

"How is business?" I asked a dealer in clothing, a day or two ago. "Dull," was the reply. "But," I returned, "it will be better after a payment." "Better after a *battle*," was the prompt and business-like reply. It gave me something to think of.

All these regions will turn into a vineyard at the least provocation, and I do not see why the sweeps of the Tennessee may not be the Rhine of the South. Grapes, large and luscious, drape the little islands, climb everything that will let them, and, the woods are purple with muscadines. Figs grow and ripen in the valleys, and here, if anywhere on the continent, the old Scripture may be verified, and the dwellers of a truth may "sit under their own vine and fig-tree."

The mountain echoes of artillery had just died away when a lively cricket of a newspaper appeared in Chattanooga, and with the daily came the newsboy—the same boy I saw curled up in a box in Nassau street, New York; the same boy that cries the "E nyn Yurn'l" on Dearborn street, Chicago; the same shrewd, sharp, old-before-his-time urchin that jumps into the clothes of his ancestors, and runs out into the world with the shell upon his back, like a young quail. If anything, he is smaller here, but then he has slipped into a pair of cavalry pantaloons when the owner was out, and he is overwhelmed in the coat of a rebel who is done with it, and altogether, resembles a shagbark walnut—more cover than kernel.

DANGER AND DESOLATION.

I saw a strange-looking party the other day, one hundred and fifty strong, attired in butternut and shirt-sleeves, mounted upon horses of every tint and action, from blue to calico, and from a limp to a lope.

Rozinante was there and the steed of Dr. Syntax, an.
so, for that matter, were Sancho Panza and "the
knight of the sorrowful countenance." Equipped with
fowling-pieces, squirrel-guns, bell-mouthed muskets that
would scatter like a flock of sheep, rifles, huge target
guns weighing thirty pounds that ought to go on
wheels, fancy little pieces, flint-lock, percussion-lock, no
lock, and the old Queen's arm, they looked as if they
had ridden right out of a dead and gone age bravely
down into our own. They proved to be men from
Middle Tennessee, who had traveled, like the Nomades,
a long journey by night, to fall in to the Federal line.

Writing of arms, have you happened to think what
a world of ingenuity has been expended upon imple-
ments of death? Take the muskets, Springfields, Aus-
trians, big Belgians, old United States; and what tribes
of carbines—Sharpe's, Merrill's, Burnside's, Gallagher's,
Joslyn's. Of the whole hundred and ten varieties of
small-arms, the Springfield rifled musket is the most
valued and trusty. Every soldier that carries one gives
it gender and makes a " Brown Bess ' of her at once.

The Tennesseans who have thus taken arms are
terrible. Shot at in their own doors, waylaid in their
own fields, their fair land made desolate around them,
their families driven homeless, shelterless from the old
roof-tree, do you wonder they never take a prisoner?

That rebels are found hanging here and there from low-limbed oaks that never bore such fruit before? That such a colloquy as this should have occurred at Murfreesboro, when the enemy's cavalry flashed through it like a shuttle?

Tennessee Cavalryman to General Ward: "We just took four prisoners, a couple of miles out of town, General, but could gain no information."

General: "Well, where are they?"

Cavalryman: "We don't know precisely. The last we saw of them they were going away into the woods with some of the boys."

The General made no comment, but in less than sixty minutes a party of Federal soldiers came into town, stating that they had just seen four "rebs" hanging from one tree.

You see, now and then in Tennessee, a quaint old house among the mountains, with the dormer windows, and the little two-seated porch, and the roofs slipping off almost down to the ground behind, like a school-girl's sun-bonnet; the oven squatted out of doors like a great mud-turtle, and the "slice" leaning against it; the well-sweep accenting the low, mossy eaves; the old-time flowers growing in the garden; the sun-flower making ready to rise; the hollyhock building its small orchestra wherein the little negroes used to bag many a bee to hear "its small and mellow horn;" earth and sky drawn very near together all around, with the spurs of the Cumberland grooved into the horizon; the clean world it all looked, and so home-like and sheltered those valleys, that it would have seemed to me next safest to being literally held in the hollow of GOD'S hand to dwell in them, had I not known that death lurked in every cedar.

Everything grows skittish in such regions except the mule. He would bray at the gates of—Dante, if a ration of corn could be made of it. I wonder what Charles Lamb—"the gentle Elia"—would have thought of it, if just entering a car at Murfreesboro, bound down, he should happen to see the side of the coach freshly peppered with shot; and if, being fairly seated, he should spy a suggestive hole in the oak panel just above his head, and on probing it should find a lazy minie-ball lying *perdu* at the bottom. What with the enemy's devilish delicacy in the shape of torpedoes which, placed beneath the rail, explode with the slightest pressure, and make kindling wood of things in a twinkling, and the swoops of hostile cavalry upon the road, running a train is nervous work, and our engineer may be pardoned for whistling "down brakes" yesterday with unusual emphasis. Something suspicious lay upon the track, and a skirmisher was sent

forward to reconnoiter. A cautious examination dis-
closed the dilapidated leg of a cavalry boot, a harmless
waif from some passing train; and with unusual
pressure to the square inch our postillion succeeded in
bringing his shy and skittish engine down to her work
again. All the eyes of all the engineers in this region
are in the fronts of their heads.

The Chattanooga, the very *Jordan* of railroads, ragged to a degree, and as full of perils as a brisk skirmish,
has done noble service, and cast aside its tattered rails
as they may, it will have "the right of way" and an
enduring Station on the historic page. The wrecks of
seven engines and one hundred and forty cars strow the
road between Nashville and Bridgeport—that capital
place for liars to tell the truth in. Verily they cannot
lie if they try. From Bridgeport to Chattanooga it is
twenty-seven miles, fifty-five miles, seventy miles. They
consume one day, three days, ten days, and it is all
true. Fancy a Potomac General ordering thirty break-
fasts and rooms for his suite at Stevenson by lightning!—Stevenson with its "Alabama House," a good
piece of property to begin a new Tophet with, should
the old one be burned out. Think of his coveting a
dinner at Bell Buckle, to which place the conductor
took fare of a passenger who profanely declared he was
bound for "the *other* place." "You'll get off at Bell

Buckle then—it s the nearest station on this road," said the conductor, and so landed him to make the rest of his journey as he could. Eight miles an hour is the passenger rate of running, and I have as yet met nobody who talked of mud-turtles, for in that eight miles you get motion enough for eighty. Worn out before the enemy had done with it, they had spiked plank upon the ties, making a broad road whereon their army wagons were driven, and the first time I passed over it, the thick double rows of beans and corn—raw succotash—growing along the rails were as good as a bill of lading as to the freight they carried.

Many of the bands that attack the trains in Tennessee are made up of desperate and abandoned citizens, whose predatory propensities are indulged under the color of war; for, they do not belong to the army at all.

General Hooker issued a two-edged sword of an order which illustrates the fact that a steel blade may be made of no tougher material than honest English. It holds residents within twenty miles upon each side of the Railroad, responsible for any damage done by guerrillas, upon the ground that the latter can only approach the line with the connivance or knowledge of such residents, and announcing further that the homes will be destroyed and the property confiscated of all who shall either by actual deed or by silence facilitate the approach of the raiders. The order cuts both ways, for it declares that under no circumstances will the surprise, abandonment or surrender of any Federal force, work or bridge along the line be pardoned.

Waiting at a desolate station in the gray of the morning, a ghostly mist hiding the river lowlands, and nothing but a ruin in sight, I saw two blots on the thick air, that took shape in a moment and loomed out of the fog a mounted picket leading a riderless horse. The saddle was stained with something heavier than dew, for it had just been emptied by a shot from an unseen hand, and the picket's comrade had fallen dead in the rank weeds. Such incidents were frequent, but a scene more eloquent of utter loneliness can hardly be imagined. It impressed me much as did another and widely different picture. Riding through a region emptied like that hapless rider's saddle of all life—the houses tumbling down in their desolateness, and the breathless chimneys standing like dumb monuments to dead households, the silence dotted now and then by a shot in the distance, ticking, perhaps, some patrolman's last minute, we halted at the foot of a great oak. Glancing up the trunk, there were slips nailed along, the rounds of a rude ladder leading to a little platform

like a hawk's nest among the foliage at the top. A
single telegraph wire was trailed up amid the leaves
like the floating thread of that brave æronaut, the field
spider. It was a deserted station where our signal
corps had made observations at the distance of fifteen
miles. The corps had moved on, the storm had swept
by, but the look-out remained.

UNDER WHICH KING?

I had read from boyhood the passage where the
orator talks so finely of the drifts of New England and
"the snows of the cotton field;" I had seen cotton
batting; heard of cotton breastworks at New Orleans
and—elsewhere, met cotton kings and attended a cotton court, but a cotton *field* was a thing in cotton I had
yet to see. Beginning with a boy's first boots, almost
all first things are memorable. Riding along one
pleasant day, I came upon a row of negroes, "a sitting
on a rail." Of different heights, their inky heads
looked like the ups and downs of a queer stave of
music, and their crooked bodies finished out the notes
with grotesque stems. This bit of a tune would have
been nowise remarkable, had not every note of it been
spotted with white. They were cotton-pickers, and

looked as if they had been out in a *storm* of it. Over
the fence beyond I beheld the cotton field. It was late
in the season and the green had faded out; the earth
showed dark beneath, and the cotton thickly sprinkled
the landscape. It was as if the first great flakes of
a snow-fall should be halted a foot or so from the
ground, and should hang obedient there. And so I
looked my first at the field whence they had picked the
fabric worn by "the girl with the blue dress on," and
gathered the folds of the star-lit flag.

I was looking upon a deposed monarch without
thinking of it; for cotton is no longer king.

I saw four hundred of the mothers of Ethiopia—and
about every one of them a *nursing* mother—"doing"
the woolens of the army in the morning shadow of the
mountain, the dingy crowd freckled a little with yellow
girls, and nothing sweet about any of them but the
laugh of the women. It almost startles you to hear
light. musical laughter from a pair of lips that might
have exuded from the india-rubber tree. I have heard
the originals of some of the songs that jumped "Jim
Crow" into much smutty immortality and clean money,
but I heard them from the poor, ragged performers
with a feeling of pain rather than amusement. "Way
down in Alabama" had lost its power to charm, and so
had the rollicking Sambos and die-away Dinahs of old

times. The nearer you get to his Guinea and Gold
Coast fathers the more elastic the negro grows. He
seems india-rubber all the way through. He resists by
yielding, and the rebound is as light and airy as a bird.
He brushes off grief as if it were a sprinkle of rain.
With him "sufficient unto the day is the evil thereof,"
and he lets the strife and fever of his life go down with
the sun.

Some hunter of the White Nile has said, "When the
sun sets all Africa dances." In Washington when Sunday comes all Africa dashes if it does not dance. It is
rampant and saltant. It is easy to see on a sunny
Sabbath what has become of the old mantle of the
aristocracy They pepper the city as from a dredge-
box, and sober it into a sort of mitigated mourning.
During the capital's troubled days in July, '64,
everybody was toned up a little but the shady side of
humanity *He,* waspish at the waist and with that
voluminous Allegheny-and-Monongahela flow of trous-
ers that suggests the idea of something pulled up by
the roots before it has done growing, sports his best,
swings his cane and cocks his hat over his north-east
eyebrow and gives the old plantation laugh. *She* is
out, beflounced, belaced and beatified, and so in pairs,
as Noah's passengers entered the ark, they go, light of
heart and of head, up and down the Avenue. Every

shade of the bleaching process is visible everywhere. Blue eyes, straight hair, and lips modeled from Apollo's 'bow here; Dinahs that might be Dianas there.

Ebony is not king.

Here at the Front nothing is exempt from the fragrance of pig-tail, cavendish, fine-cut and the wilted leaf. Everything smokes on the trains, from engine to wheel-axle. Negroes will sing, dance or cry for tobacco. Give it to them and their eyes round out to saucers of delight, and the siftings of a soldier's pocket are eagerly scraped up by the natives. Picture a lank, tallowish female of the human species, guiltless of reading, writing, soap, water and religion, who says "we'uns" and "you'uns," in a dress hanging limp, with the look and grace of a dish-cloth on a fork, and resembling in tint the inky map of the benighted portions of the globe, a piece of tobacco in her mouth and two batches of children at her heels, and you have the counterfeit presentment of a certain type of white folks, fairly pushed over the edge of decent existence, that grow among these mountains. She indulges, when she can, in the luxury called "dipping." Take a little stem of althea, chew it into a bit of a broom at one end, dip it in snuff, sweep your mouth out with it, and leave the handle sticking out of one corner, like a broom in a mop-pail, and remember all the while that

it is a woman's mouth, and you have as much of the
fashion as I mean to describe.

But the supremacy of the weed of which we have a
king's word for saying " it was the Devil sowed the
seed," is not confined to Front or race.   The blue-coat
will pay a half dollar for an ounce of it as easily as he
winks at the flash of a rifle, and many a dull, rainy
night is beguiled with the laurel-wood pipe around the
camp-fire.   Only give him light enough to see the
smoke of the sacrifice, and his troubles roll up from the
glowing bowl, melt silently into the night and vanish
away.

Amid the pagodaish adornings of the new Representative Hall, a single curious relic of the old time and
the everlasting love remains: a little russet box, that
you might put in your pocket, stands at each end of
the marble desk of the Clerk, and its use puzzles you
for a while.   But pretty soon an honorable member—
that gray father yonder—passing by, inserts a thumb
and finger in one of them, and abstracts a pinch of
something that explodes the secret in a sneeze.   They
are, of a truth, snuff-boxes, and restore, like the powder
of a rare magician, the old dead fashion and them that
followed it : you look again into the round, black
beetle of a box and see the Vanilla bean half smothered in titillating " Scotch ;" you hear the two little

knocks upon the rim as the lid is deftly lifted off and
the box extended to you with a winning grace that
even testy James of the " counter blast " would not
repulse, the dear old grandmothers of the elder Anne,
they of the spotless cap and snowy hair, are plain
before you. " Blessed are the pure in heart, for they
shall see GOD;" the beatitude was prophetic; they
have died and fulfilled it !

In the glorious days that are no more, while the
eloquent air yet trembled and grew grand with those
tones of his, as if descending angels were lighting in
the Hall, the gallant " Harry of the West" would near
the desk, they say, and with the hand but just now
beckoning to obedient Fame, would take a pinch of
" Maccaboy!" The smile with which I first saw the
brace of snuff-boxes in such a presence, has faded out
at last, for now they seem to me two little handfuls
of dust from the perished years of many a long gone
Congress. And so Sambo and Senator touch ground
together. The great capitals that cry out at you from
wall and column of the National Capitol, short and
sharp as the bark of a Scotch terrier, " Don't deface the
building! Don't spit on the floors!" ought to be an
insult to the visitor, but they are not.

Man is a ruminant and tobacco is king.

FLOWERS, POETRY AND HEROES.

When on my way down to the Front I caught my first glimpse of "the beautiful river," with its wooded shores and its graceful sweeps, and Louisville with surroundings that nature and art have conspired to beautify; saw for the first time a country under martial law, and bayonets sprouting on every corner, you will wonder that I thought less of the gleam of swords than of the flash of wit; more of the rhythmic march of poetry than of the clanking tramp of soldiers. I was thinking of a veteran editor of Kentucky. There is no city in the land that owes so much, perhaps, to a newspaper for rendering its name a sort of Western classic, and making it known far beyond all knowledge of its fashion, wealth and commercial importance, as Louisville. I need not add that the paper is the "Journal," and the editor, George D. Prentice. All through these many years, "Louisville" was a word to conjure with. Say it, and you thought of flashes of wit and thrusts of satire, of poetry the most melodious and heartful; of gallant dashes and sturdy battle, in the old time, for "Harry of the West."

And so, as speedily as I could, I found him in his sanctum. An old man with a round head and frosty hair, and an eye black, keen, sagacious, sparkling, sat there without coat or cravat, feet half-shod in slippers, dictating to an amanuensis. When my name was announced, though that of a stranger, he met me more than half way, extended both his hands, his face brightened with welcome, and he made me at home in a minute. Not a school girl's poet to look at—not slim and pale as a candle, but square-built, thick-set and compact, carrying his sixty years with a brisk and elastic step. The fire of the old days was not quite out, it only smouldered, and he talked of the brighter time long gone and the better time to come, but I could see, and there was a pain in my heart the while, that the dew was scorched off the flower of life, and the flower lay withered and worthless in his hand.

I remembered how his Journal used to open brightly upon me like the countenance of a familiar friend; how he laid his hand on the shoulders of young aspirants for literary fame like an elder brother, and bade them Godspeed; how he kindled the Western sky with a constellation of poets, leading them off with his gifted "Amelia of the West." Generous, impulsive, social, rich in the fearful gift of genius, he strowed flowers and flashed swords through the pages of the daily press and never halted to gather them up. Time robbed him, year by year, of some sweet grace of youth; and there came a day when the Muse stood silent and pensive on his threshold. The friends that had cheered him on fell away from him; the men that had battled with him and loved him wearied and slept; the women whose bright eyes brightened at his wit and softened with his song, had gone away to be seen no more. And so the old man died, and so in his own words—

"Within the deep,
Still chambers of the heart, a specter dim,
Whose tones are like the wizard voice of Time,
Heard from the tomb of ages, points its cold
And solemn finger to the beautiful
And holy visions that have passed away,
And left no shadow of their loveliness
On the dead waste of life. That specter lifts
The coffin-lid of Hope, and Joy, and Love,
And bending mournfully above the pale,
Sweet forms, that slumber there, scatters dead flowers
O'er what has passed to nothingness.
                        Remorseless Time .
Fierce spirit of the glass and scythe !—what power
Can stay him in his silent course, or melt
His iron heart to pity ? On, still on
He presses, and forever."

I had an old song brightened up for me, one day—a doleful tale of a bride who played "hide-and-seek," between one generation and another, on a Christmas day, and descended to people who *should* have been her grand-children, in "an old oak chest." I saw the burden of that song in Alabama and Tennessee, hanging in round green clusters upon oaks impoverished of any leaves of their own. The effect of those globes of verdure was singular enough to arrest my attention even in the midst of graver things for thought, and to provoke an inquiry, and the answer was the burden of that identical song:

"Oh, the Mistletoe Bough !"

In vividness and variety, the autumnal colorings of Southern woods far surpass our own. It may be that the keen shafts of green thrust up here and there serve to set off "the coat of many colors." You can see cones of hills that burn like strange and wonderful gems, and would put out the light in Sindbad's Valley of Diamonds; great trees whose entire foliage resembles a single crimson or golden flower, so evenly and wonderfully are the tints laid on, and all you can think of, as you look, is not a trunk of a tree bearing its crown of painted leaves, but a stem lightly lifting its one majestic blossom up before the Lord. I saw such

trees and woods touched and set on fire with the
sinking sun, last night. I had read, in an old volume,
of the Burning Bush, but I never saw it until then.
How they did kindle and flash up, as Day walked
along the tops of the forest! I believe that if ever I
have to take up the blind man's "but not to me returns
day nor the sweet approach of even or morn," that
scene will come back again and again—one of the
brightest and loveliest pictures in memory. I pray all
practical men and women to pardon me for strowing
this paragraph very broadly with such trifles as leaves
and flowers. But I cannot help thinking, with another,
tha' the Lord loves to look at them Himself. Would
anybody have liked it better, do you think, had I told
him that I saw oak leaves, as early as September, more
richly colored than any I saw last night?—costlier far
than the dye of Tyre?

And speaking of flowers, I have seen soldiers go
into battle with a rose or a geranium leaf carefully
pinned upon the breast. Does anybody think the love
of a posy made against their manhood—that they were
any less the hero? It was the touch of the same
poetic feeling that, toned up and glorified, makes epics
—that made Sergeant Williams, the color-bearer of
Company D, 51st Illinois, when the flag was shot clean
away at Chicamauga, grasp the standard and cry out,

"the staff is left yet, boys—it's enough to fight by!"
A soldier of the 79th Illinois was struck by the fragment of a shell upon the hip, and the next minute a
musket-ball penetrated a case containing the portraits
of his wife and two children, and lay there as harmlessly amid that little family of shadows as a trinket
in a woman's bosom.

"Do you know," said he, "that for all that lump of
lead left the picture not worth a Continental I wouldn't
swap it for a farm? It isn't so much, you see, that my
life was saved by anything as that it was saved by *such*
a thing—my wife and babies, and they a thousand
miles off all the while!" Was there not a vein in that
man's soul of the sort of stuff that makes lyrics?

Ah, many a rude and sturdy trooper in the old wars
of York and Lancaster fought as much for an emblem,
for the white rose or the red, as if it had been a love-
gift from the woman of his heart.

Going up Mission Ridge, Colonel Wiley, of the 41st
Ohio. fell terribly wounded at the first line of rifle-pits,
and General Hazen rode up, with the words, "I hope
you are not badly wounded." "Do you think we'll
make it?" asked the Colonel. "I do," was the reply. .
"That's enough," said the gallant officer; "I can stand
this!"—and there he lay bleeding and content, and
the tide of battle went on. What, but a grand ideal

inspired that man and summoned back his ebbing soul? As he lay there with closed eyes he saw the 41st roll over the height like a blue wave, "distinct like a billow" in that "one like the sea."

At Shiloh a white dove, bewildered by the thunder, flew in and out amid the clouds of the battle, and at last fluttered panting down upon the wheel of a gun. It was a strange place for the emblem of purity and peace; it belonged to the white flag and not to the red. An artilleryman captured it in his grimy hands, caressed it a moment, freed it, and in an instant it was lost in the storm. Had that caressing touch been translated into English speech can you doubt it would have been a word of love and memory melodious as a little song? Had that bird flown with the captor's thought, can you doubt it would have fluttered at last at a window of the gunner's far-off home?

The story of the war contains abundant proof that the negro may possess a yet nobler quality than mere animal courage; that he can touch the heroic height that makes life grand and death a poem. Very seldom indeed, for in any race the sparrows are many, but the eagles are few. Do you not think the black color-bearer, who planted the flag on the enemy's works, and who, though brought down by a shot, yet held it flying clear of the earth, and when the recall was sounded, crept away bleeding and faint, still bearing the flag aloft, and when he had brought it off in safety, sinking down with the exulting words, "I never let it touch the ground!"—do you not think that man had at least one foot on the pedestal where stands the white Apollo of the superior race?

A SOLDIER'S "TILL."

Is the reader old-fashioned enough to know what a "till" is? That bit of a chest in one corner of the bureau where they used to deposit the little trinkets of memory—the odds and ends of times past; fragments of Susan's wedding-dress and Jessy's shroud, a lock of the baby's hair that heard the Saviour's sweet injunction, "suffer little children to come unto me and forbid them not"—heard it and went; two or three beads from a broken string, two or three letters in faded ink. Now, this letter is a "till," filled with trifles from camp and field.

———

From November 24th, 1863, to April 24th, 1864, of one thousand and twenty-six who had been laid in the Soldiers' Rest at Chattanooga, one hundred and sixty-seven were killed on the field of battle. When, with

my finger running down the long lines of names, I came
to the end of the roll of honor, and my thought rested
at one hundred sixty-seven, will you believe that I
could not credit the count, and went over all the pages
again, sure that I should find a few more, opposite
whose names—with a running pen, and a flourish now
and then—the clerks had written the three words,
"*Killed in action.*" But the sixty-eighth was not
there! There it was: one hundred and sixty-seven fell
on the field; three hundred and seventy-eight died from
wounds; five hundred and forty-five in all, from bullets;
only fifty-three per cent. of the thousand and twenty-
six. And what of the four hundred and eighty-one?
Hardships, exposure, the wasting fever, "the slings and
arrows" of rheumatism, and all the ills of the empty
box that stands wide open in the midst of camps, but
at whose bottom is "Hope, the charmer," still, even
as she lingered there in the old time. The battle
ended, the Surgeon's duty done, how does the work of
Physician and Sanitary Commission rise almost to the
dignity of the army's salvation!

The battle is the red blossom of War, but the roots,
dark and bitter, run beneath ten thousand tents and
cabins, creep through unnumbered wards of hospitals,
and feel their way like the fingers of a hand in all this
ground we tread upon, save that great, solemn acre,
rich in Soldiers dead—the acre of the living GOD.

If anybody thinks that when our men are stricken upon the field they fill the air with cries and groans, till it shivers with such evidence of agony, he greatly errs. An arm is shattered, a leg carried away, a bullet pierces the breast, and the soldier sinks down silently upon the ground, or creeps away, if he can, without murmur or complaint; falls as the sparrow falls, speechlessly, and like that sparrow, I earnestly believe, falls not without the Father. The dying horse gives out his fearful utterance of almost human suffering, but the mangled rider is dumb. The crash of musketry, the crack of rifles, the roar of guns, the shriek of shells, the rebel whoop, the Federal cheer, and that indescribable undertone of grinding, rumbling, splintering sound, make up the voices of the battle-field.

Among the curiosities of army life is this: dress eighty thousand men pretty nearly alike, and everybody resembles his neighbor, and nobody looks like himself. Take those men and sprinkle a half-section, as they say in the West, pretty thickly with them; put them under the big umbrellas of the camps, chink a little town full of them till every house swarms like a hive in June, set them all in the usual motion of army life and then begin to look for your next best friend, and I wish you joy of your journey; you might better be "Japhet in search of his father." Perhaps you may remember having passed a familiar friend who was reclining in the chair with his face upturned, as is the fashion of those who come under the barber's hands—passed without recognizing him. Of course it was the unwonted position that gave him the look of a stranger, the shadows fell in new places, and the effect was a new impression. You would be struck with this in looking down upon the faces turned towards heaven after a battle, either on the field or in the hospital; the light falls squarely down : no shadows under the brow, no shading beneath the chin, and the whole face so clears up, softens and grows delicate, that you may be looking upon a friend and not know it. Death, I think, generally impairs the beauty of women, but it sometimes makes homely men wonderfully handsome.

———————

Did you ever go to a soldier's harvest? A dozen mule teams are geared up, an hundred men detailed, and, with tin kettles swung aloft from their bayonets, away they go over the mountains, to a broad corn forest of an hundred and fifty acres. It is splendid corn; the ears are as long as a Marshal's baton, close set, with kernels as clean, white and firm as the teeth that

Richard was born with. The arms are stacked. Two hours finish the business. Two sabres do duty as corn cutters. and the rustling ranks succumb. The boys follow after, gather up the forage, load the wagons, and away moves the train *en route* for camp, with the strangest harvest-songs and the wildest surroundings. No children's happy shouts follow the reapers; no women smile a welcome home. No harvest cheer makes glad the closing day. It is one of those scenes conjured up by the stern necessities of war, to which let all men pray we may evermore be strangers.

I got in good company on the Tennessee one day, being a fellow-voyager with General Hooker's horse "White Surrey," ridden by him in no end of battles, and I must say I have been in worse company with fewer feet. Large, strong, short in the back, broad in the breast; not so very clean-limbed, but then all muscle and endurance, and a noble bearer for his noble burden. He stood upon a barge towed beside the steamer, and when the engine gave a shrill, loonish cry above his head, instead of bounding about and acting like a coward, he looked quietly up with those great, wide-open eyes of his; and when the steam rushed out

from the escape pipe almost under his nose, with a
fierce hiss that made the groom start, he just turned an
eye inquiringly downward, his nostrils dilating a little,
but he never stirred out of his tracks. He is a fearless,
generous creature, worthy the respect even of a Major-
General. It is no new statement, perhaps, but then
you have rich opportunities for verifying it in the
Army: horses do not always "keep their distance"
from mankind. Some of them meet the best of men
full half-way in almost every noble thing except a
living soul.

The poetry of many a scene will slip out of it if you
only wait long enough. I wish you could have been
with me this lovely morning, for you would have seen a
line of poetry written in dark blue across the plain from
the base of Lookout, one and a half miles. It might
have been a hedge with rich, deep foliage, blossomed
out at intervals with flowers, only it was not there last
night. You might think so still, but the line is growing
before your eyes. As you look, an electric light flickers
along the blue, even as the lightning played upon
Roman spears in Cæsar's time; it is the flash of bur-
nished arms in the sunshine. As you look, men by
companies and regiments are born from the narrow

breadth; the flowers are those whose fibers feel out the graves of them that sleep. As you listen, the swell from band after band rolls in, and on they come. And now the words of Reginald Heber's sweet, old song, escaped from the book, are written out before you in War's bold autograph, and

> "You see them on their winding way,
>   About their ranks the sunbeams play."

Nearer they come, the music intermits, and you have the heavy tread of men, and the tinkling of four thousand tin cups, like a whole Chaldea of bell-wethers. Heber slips back into the book again, poetry exhales, and you have the prose of six regiments of fighting men, the 120th, 123d, 124th, 128th, 129th and 130th Indiana, of General Hovey's Division, the vanguard of the twenty thousand on the way from that same State—new men, indeed, but worthy guardians of the old fame. Five pairs of flags, gay as the wings of butterflies, went glittering by, that never rose and fell on the surges of battle, and one poor rag, tattered by the tempest, borne proudly in their midst; the dyes of the dyer were dim, but the death of the heroes had made the tints sublime. Your heart would have warmed to the old flag as it never could warm to the new. This was nothing but silk yet, at so many dollars a yard, but

that had gone up the ladder of meaning, like the
angels in the vision of the patriarch in the wilderness—
it had become COLORS. The productions of Indiana
have grown grand. By what stately marches she steps
into glory forever: hogs, hominy, horses, Hoosiers and
Heroes.

The blessed rain washed down the smoky air for the
first time in two months, and came to the men in the
trenches before Petersburg in July, 1864, like a bene-
diction. · The little gopher holes they had scooped out
with cup and bayonet ceased, for a few hours, to be
wallows of ashes, and when the great, clean drops came
down, sharpshooters opened both eyes; by common
consent there was a lull in the scattering gusts of leaden
rain, and our fellows straightened up in their burrows,
and showed themselves to the waistbands, and doffed
their broad-brimmed hats, for such of them as can
read, believed the saying that the LORD sendeth His
rain upon the evil as well as upon the good. The
patter upon the baking earthworks and the tinkle
upon the tin kettles were about as sweet as the bugle-
note of victory, and some of the boys, recalling a
snatch of an old psalm tune, sang, albeit the spot

where they lay is not half as much like a garden as it is like a kennel,

> " The LORD into his garden comes,"

and a hearty voice burst out with,

> "Refreshing showers of grace divine
> From JESUS flow to every vine,
> And make the dead revive,
> And make the dead re-vi-ve "—

Crack! *Ping*—the enemy are short of gratitude; there comes a bullet! and again there are ridges of earth and not a man in sight; every head is sowed like a kernel of corn in a drill.

A single Congressional District has sent more men to the war for the Union than Washington led over the Delaware; six times as many as went up to Bunker Hill and glory on that long-gone day in June. The battle of Tippecanoe, that wrought one man's name and fame into imperishable story, was fought with seven hundred men—less than a round regiment. What would the old Continentals have thought of such a veneering of men and iron: this April day, 1864, the

Federal line extends from Huntsville, on its extreme right, along the Tennessee to Chattanooga, the center, and thence onward, our left resting on Knoxville, and showing a grand iron front of two hundred and ten miles, ready at every point to do battle. Beyond our left, a thinner line extends for twenty miles, and beyond Huntsville another away to Memphis, presenting an impregnable barrier to infantry, unless in strong force, and through which only cavalry would venture to break. Think of that front with its two hundred mile sweep, swelling out into fortifications, like the muscular ridges of a strong arm, the rear clamped to it by iron bars all along, thus placed in daily and bodily communication, and made one by the instinctive flash of the telegraph!

War has become an exact science. Take Fort Negley at Nashville, as it was, with its glittering howitzers, its Parrots, those mighty birds of prey, its crowded magazines, its shot and shell, its salient angles—a grand star of earth and stone resting on the summit of the hill, with a radiating power of thunder and death that commands the approaches in all directions. The distance to each visible grove and eminence has been accurately measured and mapped out upon paper in diverging lines from the Fort, giving the length of the swing of the iron hammers. So the science of War, like the arts of Peace, has been developed with the accuracy of mathematics, and quickened by lightning and by steam, till smoky battery and dusty harvester move to the compound table of time and space that characterizes the age:

SIXTY SECONDS MAKE ONE . . . . MILE.

Thus I have turned over the trifles in the "till" and selected a little handful, and for the last let it be a pleasant picture and a mention of the dear old neighbors of my country home, who donned the blue and went away, some to wounds and sorrow and death, but all to honor and duty and a loving memory. "Winter quarters" does not mean ragged tents crackling with frost, and snow-drifts in the corners, but something as comfortable as a Christmas pie. Take the most natty bit of a log cabin you ever saw, give it a toy of a chimney, as cunning as a swallow's nest, a close-fitting door, and a couple of hands' breadths of a window beside it, as if the alert little cottage slept with one eye open, and you have the picture of thousands of soldiers' homes in Alabama and Tennessee. I have ridden through dozens of such villages within the month just ended, strown all along upon the mountain sides and in the valleys, and there is about them an air of comfort as warm as a hearty welcome. Now and then, a hamlet wears decidedly a city look. One has its doors numbered and porches before them. Indeed, I saw several tenements that would have graced elegant grounds as rustic cottages; and one little Gothic structure, midway between Chattanooga and Kelly's Ferry, should have its portrait in some volume of " Rural Architecture."

It was in such a beautiful encampment that I last saw the 105th Illinois, and no better material ever went to the Front from the Prairie State—of such stuff as made the 34th and 79th Illinois, that stood in their tracks and fired eighty rounds without a backward step. Daniel Dustin, its Colonel, won and wore a star; its Lieutenant-Colonel was Henry F. Vallette; Major, E. F. Dutton; Surgeons, H. S. Potter—who at once assumed Brigade duties, was killed on the field, and when they made a grave for him they laid in it one of nature's truest noblemen—A. Waterman and G. W. Briggs. Its Captains were of the sort that lead a forlorn hope without faltering. The rank and file were like a field of wheat, the bearded grain and the flowers that grow between, stalwart manhood and youth, with the springing step. I can count with a glance of the eye from the threshold of my old cottage home, in the little village of Wheaton, thirteen dwellings, and from every one of them soldiers, sometimes in pairs, have departed; struggling in the terrible days of the Potomac; crowding on into the rough weather of northern Georgia. The old enthusiasm that kindled the homes of Du Page into altars of sacrifice seems to me most like the song of bugles in a dream.

Time passed, and again I went in sight of the little mountain city of the 105th. It was dismantled and lone. The triumphal curves of evergreen had faded and fallen; the blue smokes no longer threaded their way up from the little chimneys; the smooth streets were deserted. Where were the groups of blue I had seen; the gay laugh I had heard; the glittering arms that flashed on my sight? Fleeting as a dream, the regiment had slung the knapsack and beat the drum and gone on towards the terrible Front. Wading in deep waters, falling on fields of red fame, languishing in hospitals—who shall read the record of those strong, manly ranks without a throb of pain and pride?—and through all, fighting for the homes in Kendall, De Kalb and Du Page, the gardens of Illinois. And to-day I call out of the loneliness, and as so many times before, so now out of my heart I bid ye, old friends of the 105th Illinois, hail and farewell!

ENDED.

It was a day in later autumn. In a fire-place, laid in mud like a swallow's nest, its wild sprout of a chimney budded out at the top with a barrel, and looking like a monument to the last bricklayer, burned an old-fashioned fire built of wood from Mission Ridge, and crackling with feeble memories of the musketry of the grand old battle. The drums, with their flutters and cheers, their single ruffles and double drags, like the wicked, had "ceased from troubling;" Bonaparte had got over the Rhine; "Nancy Dawson" slipped out at the shrill end of the fifes, and the bugles had warbled good night.

Again it is a day in later autumn. The trees have struck their colors to grace the dying year. This wood, now burning at my feet, never shook in the tempest of battle. These old Chenango hills never mocked the thunder of the shotted gun. The robin in the mountain ash sits silent mid the rubies, and takes his last supper in the chilly North. The songs of the summer are over and gone. I turn these leaves as Hebrew children read, back to the book's beginning, and every chapter is a hook whereon to hang a memory—one glorious, another sad, but all imperishable. Clear, earnest eyes and faces brave and grand, no other reader sees, look at me from the pages as I turn; some with a dying glance, and some with a bright smile of friendly recognition. The graves are made; the sword is sheathed; the musket hangs dumb upon its wooden hooks; the white blessings of peace like lilies strow the water and blossom along the land like daisies in the June pastures. Then

"Farewell the plumed troop and the big wars!"

Among the mountains, for the first time in my life, I have seen clouds *born*. Breaths of vapor, like smokes from camp-fires, wreathe their way up above the tops of the trees in one place and another, looking thin and pale in the early morning. You have not the least idea what will come of it all; but, by and by, they melt into one, assume volume and color, and before you think of it, a cloud, made up of a whole family of the little breaths, is sailing grandly away. Thunder is born of it. There are clouds that are born of the thunder. May they never again darken the valley or mantle the mountain in this our day, till War in the new world shall be a calm and pensive memory, far off and beautiful as the thought of a crimson and golden sunset in the WEST.

THE WORLD ON WHEELS, and Other Sketches.—

By BENJ. F. TAYLOR. Illustrated. 1 vol., 12mo. Price, $1.50.

"Full of humor and sharp as a Damascus blade."—*Presbyterian, Phila.*

"The pen-pictures of B. F. Taylor are among the most brilliant and eccentric productions of the day. They are like the music of Gottschalk played by Gottschalk himself; or like sky-rockets that burst in the zenith, a d fall in showers of fiery rain. They are word-wonders, reminding us of necromancy, with the dazzle and bewilderment of their rapid succession."—*Chicago Tribune.*

"Reader, do you want to laugh? Do you want to cry? Do you want to climb the Jacob's ladder of imagination, and dwell among the clouds of fancy for a little while at least? Do you? Then get B. F. Taylor's World on Wheels, read it, and experience sensations you never felt before! * * It is a book of 'word pictures,' a string of pearls, the very poesy of thought."—*The Christian, St. Louis.*

"Another of Benj. F. Taylor's wonderful word painting books. * * In purity of style and originality of conception, Taylor has no superiors in this country. The book before us is a gem in every way. It is quaint, poetical, melodious, unique, rare as rare flowers are rare. He has an exquisite faculty of illustration that is unsurpassed in the whole range of American literature."—*St. Louis Dispatch.*

OLD-TIME PICTURES and SHEAVES of RHYME.

By BENJ. F. TAYLOR. Red line edition, small quarto, silk cloth, with eight fine full page illustrations.

Price --$2 00
The same, full gilt edges and gilt side---------------------- 2 50

JOHN G. WHITTIER *writes :*—"It gives me pleasure to see the poems of B. F. Taylor issued by your house in a form worthy of their merit. Such pieces as the '*Old Village Choir,*' '*The Skylark,*' '*The Vane on the Spire,*' and '*June,*' deserve their good setting. * * I do not know of anyone who so well reproduces the home scenes of long ago. There is a quiet humor that pleases me."

"Unless it be Whittier, we know of no American poet so sweet, tender and gentle in his lyrics as B. F. Taylor. No writer of to-day sings the praises of rural life and scenery as eloquently, and we do not wonder that many of his poems have become classic. The holiday volume of his happy verses, OLD TIME PICTURES AND SHEAVES OF RHYME is a very eloquent and daintily bound volume, and comes from that growing and reliable publishing house of the West, S. C. Griggs & Company, of Chicago. Taking up this handsomely printed book, we have to linger on the delightful imagery and graceful diction of its pages, glowing as they are with pure and tender thoughts, and the earnest, indescribable music of sunny fields and rural joys. * * No one can read it but will be the better for so doing."— *The Albany Morning Express.*

GETTING ON IN THE WORLD; or, Hints on Success in Life.

— By WM. MATHEWS, LL.D., Professor of English Literature, etc., in the University of Chicago. Beautifully printed and handsomely bound.

Price, 1 vol., 12mo., Cloth........$2 25 | Half calf binding, gilt top.......$3 50
The same, gilt edges .... 2 50 | Full calf, gilt edges............. 5 00

CONTENTS:— *Success and Failure — Good and Bad Luck — Choice of a Profession — Physical Culture — Concentration — Self-Reliance — Originality in Aims and Methods — Attention to Details — Practical Talent — Decision — Manner — Business Habits — Self-Advertising — The Will and the Way — Reserved Power — Economy of Time — Money, its Use and Abuse — Mercantile Failures — Over-Work and Under-Rest — True and False Success.*

" A book in the highest degree attractive, * * and which will be sure to *pay in dollars and cents* many times over the cost of the work, and the time devoted to its perusal."—*Lockport Journal, New York.*

" It is sound, morally and mentally. It gives no one-sided view of life; it does not pander to the lower nature; but it is high-toned, correctly toned throughout. * * There is an earnestness and even eloquence in this volume which makes the author appear to speak to us from the living page. It reads like a speech. There is an electric fire about every sentence."—*Episcopal Register, Philadelphia.*

" There is no danger of speaking in too high terms of praise of this volume. As a work of art it is a gem. As a counselor it speaks the wisdom of the ages. As a teacher it illustrates the true philosophy of life by the experience of eminent men of every class and calling. It warns by the story of signal failures, and encourages by the record of triumphs that seemed impossible. It is a book of facts and not of theories. The men who have succeeded in life are laid under tribute, and made to divulge the secret of their success. They give vastly more than 'hints;' they make a revelation. They show that success lies not in luck, but in pluck. Instruction and inspiration are the chief features of the work which Prof. Mathews has done in this volume."—*Christian Era, Boston.*

THE GREAT CONVERSERS, and Other Essays.

— By WM. MATHEWS, LL.D., author of " Getting On in the World."

1 volume, 12mo., 306 pages, with Map, price.................$1 75

" As fascinating as anything in fiction."—*Concord Monitor.*

" These pages are crammed with interesting facts about literary men and literary work."—*New York Evening Mail.*

" They are written in that charming and graceful style, which is so attractive in this author's writings, and the reader is continually reminded by their ease and grace of the elegant compositions of Goldsmith and Irving."—*Boston Transcript.*

" Twenty essays, all treating lively and agreeable themes, and in the easy, polished and sparkling style that has made the author famous as an essayist. * * The most striking characteristic of Prof. Mathews' writing is its wonderful wealth of illustration. * * One will make the acquaintance of more authors in the course of a single one of his essays than are probably to be met with in the same limited space anywhere else in the whole realm of our literature."—*The Chicago Tribune.*

PRE-HISTORIC RACES OF THE UNITED STATES.

By J. W. FOSTER, LL.D., Author of " The Physical Geography of the Mississippi Valley," etc. 415 pages, crown 8vo, with a large number of illustrations.

Price, cloth	$3 50
Half calf binding, gilt top	6 00
Full calf, gilt edges	7 50

" One of the best and clearest accounts we have seen of those grand monuments of a forgotten race."—*London Saturday Review.*

" The reader will find it more fascinating than his last favorite novel."— *Eclectic Magazine, N. Y.*

" The book is literally crowded with astonishing and valuable facts."— *Boston Post.*

" It is an elegant volume and a valuable contribution to the subject. * * * Contains just the kind of information in clear, compressed and intelligible form, which is adapted to the mass of readers."—*Appleton's Popular Science Monthly.*

" The book is typographically perfect, and with its admirable illustrations and convenient index is really elegant and a sort of luxury to possess and read. * * Dr. Foster's style reminds us of Tyndall and Proctor, at their best. * * He goes over the ground, inch by inch, and accumulates information of surprising interest and importance, bearing on this subject, which he gives in his crowded but most instructive and entertaining chapters in a thoroughly scientific but equally popular way. We have marked whole pages of his book for quotation, and finally from sheer necessity have been compelled to put the whole volume in quotation marks, as one of the few books that are indispensable to the student, and scarcely less important for the intelligent reader to have at hand for reference."—*Golden Age, New York.*

A MANUAL OF GESTURE. — With over 100 Figures,

embracing a complete system of Notation, with the Principles of Interpretation and Selections for Practice. By Prof. A. M. BACON.

Price	$1 75

" Prof. Bacon has given us a work that, in thoroughness and practical value, deserves to rank among the most remarkable books of the season. There has in fact, been no work on the subject yet offered to the public which approaches it for exhaustiveness and completeness of detail. * * It is of the utmost value, not merely to students, but to lawyers, clergymen, teachers, and public speakers, and its importance as an assistant in the formation of a correct and appropriate style of action can hardly be over-estimated."—*The Philadelphia Inquirer.*

" Prof. Bacon's Manual seems expressly arranged for the help of those who study alone and have undertaken self-instruction in the art of persuasive delivery. The work in the hands of our ministry, well studied, would have the effect of emphasizing the living words of the Gospel all over the land, and making them two-edged with meaning."—*The Chicago Pulpit.*

PHILOSOPHY OF THE PLAN OF SALVATION.—

By Rev. J. B. WALKER, D.D., with an Introductory Essay by CALVIN E. STOWE, D.D. A new edition, with supplementary chapter by the author. Sixty-seventh thousand. 1 vol. 12mo. Price, $1.50.

" Though written with great simplicity, it is evidently the production of a master mind. * * and few works are more adapted to bring skeptics of a certain class to a stand. * * It is the disclosure of the actual process of mind through which the author passes, from the dark regions of doubt and infidelity to the clear light and conviction of a sound and heartfelt belief of the truth as it is in Jesus.

" There is in many parts of this treatise, a force of argument and a power of conviction almost resistless.

" It is a work of extraordinary power. * * We think it is *more likely to lodge an impression in the human conscience, in favor of the divine authority of Christianity*, than any work of the modern press."— *London Evangelical Magazine, England.*

" No single volume we ever read has been so satisfactory a demonstration of the truth of religion, or has had so strong a controlling influence over our habits of thought. * * No better book can be put into the hands of the honest and intellectual skeptic. It is overwhelmingly convincing to reason, and leaves the doubter nothing but his passions and prejudices to bolster him up. * * Every minister's library should have a copy."— *The Methodist Protestant, Baltimore.*

" It fills a place in theological literature which no other book does. It is the style of the argument which gives power, impressiveness, and perennial freshness to this production. * * We have found in pastoral experience that we could place no better uninspired book than this in the hands of intelligent doubters, or in the hands of new converts, for their aid and guidance. Those who are not familiar with it, will do well to procure a copy and study it carefully. It is worth more than some large libraries to those who read for their profiting."— *The Christian at Work, New York.*

THE DOCTRINE OF THE HOLY SPIRIT; Or Philosophy of the Divine Operation in the Redemption of Man.—Being volume second of " The Philosophy of the Plan of Salvation."

By Rev. J. B. WALKER, D.D. Fourth edition, revised and enlarged. Price, $1.50.

" The author's former able works have prepared the public for the rich treasures of thought in this volume. It is a book of foundation principles, and deals in the verities of the gospel as with scientific facts. It is an unanswerable argument in behalf of Christ's life, mission, and doctrine, and especially rich in its teachings concerning the office and work of the Spirit. No volume has lately issued from the press which brings so many timely truths to the public attention. While it is metaphysical and thorough, it is also clever, forceful, winning for its grand truth's sake, and *every way readable*. The author has wrought a great work for the Christian Church, and *every minister and teacher should arm himself with strong weapons* by perusing the arguments of this book. It is printed and bound in the exquisite style of all publications which issue from Messrs. S. C. Griggs & Co.'s establishment."— *Methodist Recorder, Pittsburgh.*